I0818035

ANONYME

A CLAYTON MUTTLER NOVEL

GREGORY MCEWAN

ANONYME

A CLAYTON MUTTLER NOVEL

ISBN-13: 978-0-9940087-5-6

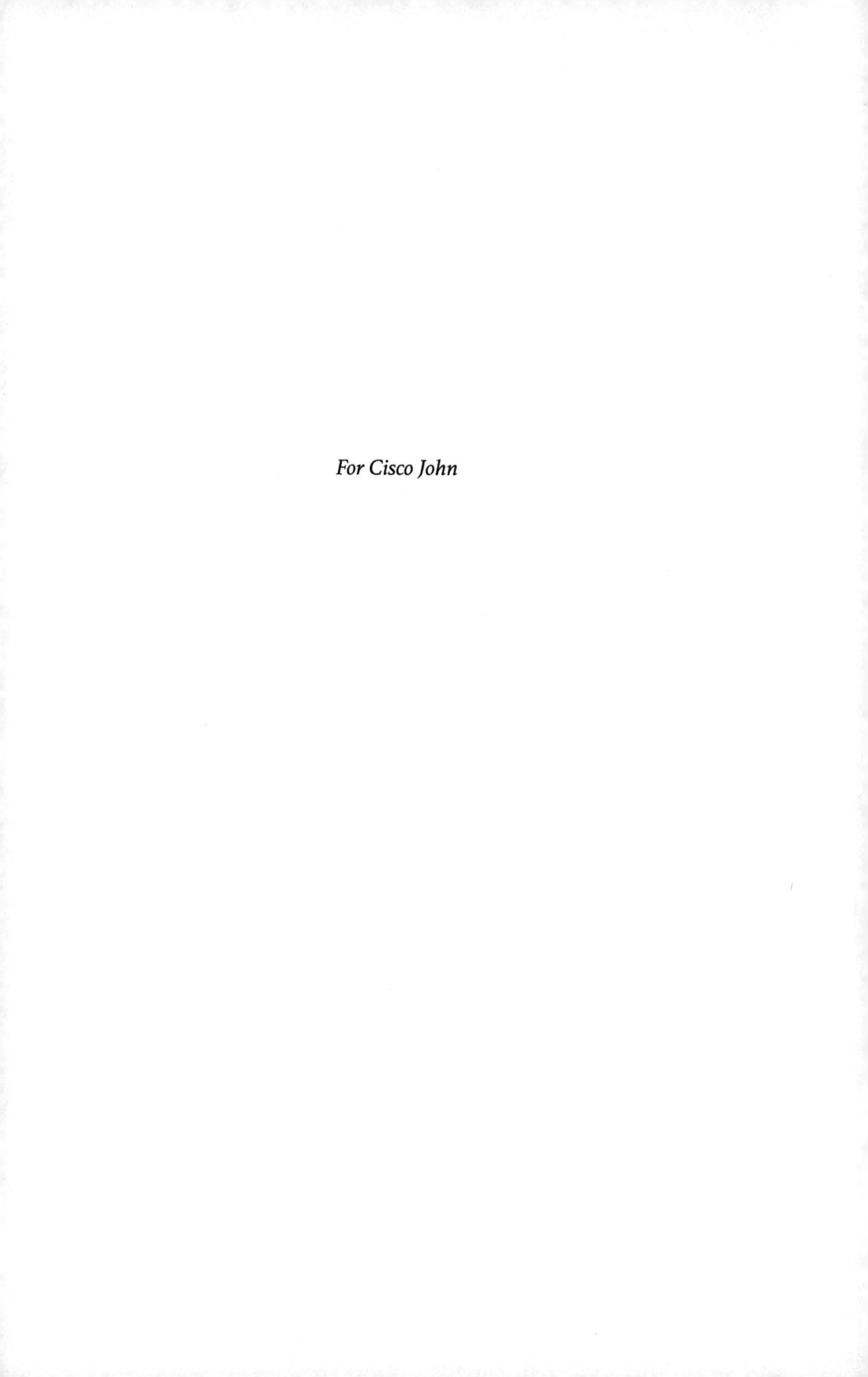

For Cisco John

PROLOGUE

Digging a grave at night was tedious work. The man leaned on the shovel, breath heaving in the frozen air. His gloves were stiff with frost, offering little protection against the biting cold. Midnight had draped the landscape in silence, an emptiness so complete it made his pulse sound deafening in his ears.

No one for miles. No witnesses.

He flexed his fingers, wincing as the numbed joints cracked. The wind slithered through the trees, whispering over the shallow pit at his feet. It had taken him an hour to dig, but he knew it should have been deeper.

With a sigh, he tossed the shovel aside and turned to the body lying a few paces away. Even in death, she looked fragile—her limbs limp, her face slack, those green eyes frozen wide in shock. For a moment, he stared, the thrill of the kill still humming in his veins.

Taking lives was exhilarating. Disposing of them? A chore.

Pulling his gloves back on, he knelt and lifted her into his arms. Dead weight always felt heavier, but he carried her with ease. The cold had already begun to set in, stiffening her joints. Lowering her carefully into the grave, he hesitated. Then, almost tenderly, he dragged his gloved fingers over her lids, closing her eyes.

No dirt in those eyes.

By morning, fresh snowfall would bury any trace of her. He gave the grave a final pat with the back of his shovel, smoothing the surface. Then he turned and trudged toward his truck, boots crunching in the frost.

He hated this part. The cleanup. The waiting. The knowledge that it was never enough.

Reaching the truck, he lifted the trunk and tossed the shovel inside. His gaze snagged on a small object resting beside it—a simple gold wedding band. He picked it up, rolling it between his fingers. Too small to fit him, but that didn't matter. He always kept something. A token. A reminder.

Slipping it into his pocket, he slammed the trunk shut, harder than necessary.

Practice. He needed more practice.

Sliding into the driver's seat, he turned the key, the truck coughing to life. He gripped the wheel, replaying the night in his mind. Had he left anything behind? No. He was careful. Precise. Still, unease gnawed at him.

It wasn't perfect.

And that meant he'd have to do it again.

PART I

1

The package arrived promptly at noon, just as promised. Her husband, Sam, was away on a business trip, making it the perfect time for her delivery. Evelyn glared at the elegant label bearing her full name, embossed in gold. She took a deep breath, trying to let her excitement drown out the guilt that tugged at her. Everything about the square velvet box, tied with a black satin ribbon, exuded luxury.

She had been sitting at the dining table for what felt like hours, staring at the box since retrieving it from the doorstep. "Goddammit, Evelyn, what the hell are you doing?" she muttered to herself, shaking her head.

Evelyn and Sam had been married for two years and were trying to start a family. As always, Sam found a way to blame her for their struggles. A familiar wave of frustration welled up inside her as she ran her fingers over the lid of the box. She felt foolish for letting Monica talk her into this.

The box wasn't heavy but was slightly larger than a standard hatbox. Its delivery hadn't come through the local post—it had been chauffeured directly to her door. Yet there had been no knock, no call from the concierge, no warning of its arrival. The only thing Evelyn knew was that the package would be outside her door at noon, exactly as promised. That was all the information she had received after registering online and paying five thousand dollars.

Evelyn reached for the ribbon and tugged it slightly, nearly loosening the knot, before pulling her hand away. She rubbed her eyes, a half-smile forming as she fixed her gaze on the black box.

Her cell phone rang, startling her.

"Hey, did you get it?" Monica's eagerness made Evelyn chuckle.

"I can't believe you talked me into this, Monica."

"Girl, you need to finish what you started. You can't doubt yourself with stuff like this." Monica's voice was lively, music playing faintly in the background, making it hard for Evelyn to focus.

"You're the one who started it."

"Seriously, Evie! Did you open the box? Which one did they send you?"

"I don't know, Monica! I haven't opened it yet."

"Well, you can't cancel now. No refunds, remember?"

Evelyn sighed, the urge to weep building in her chest. She sat there, eyes closed, listening to Monica ramble on.

"Oh, Evie, trust me—you need this. It'll make you feel better." Monica's tone had shifted, more serious now. She knew how emotional Evelyn could get. "Only you can take control of your life, girl. Keep your head up. Now, I'm gonna hang up. Just open the fucking box!"

Evelyn opened her eyes, staring at the box. Monica was right. She needed to open the damned thing. She needed to be ready. Her appointment was at 8:00 PM the following day.

SHE'D DONE THIS THE DAY BEFORE, WHEN THE PACKAGE FIRST ARRIVED, BUT Evelyn couldn't resist looking at the contents of the box one more time. She knew it wouldn't be the last.

It was the day of her appointment, and though she was just a couple of years shy of her thirtieth birthday, Evelyn felt like a giddy schoolgirl. In a few hours, she would walk several blocks to the designated pickup location, carrying the box and its contents. She was to wear a party dress—something dark and simple. Bright colours and sparkle weren't permitted.

Her gaze lingered on the embossed name at the top of the card: Evelyn Greene. She frowned. Evelyn hated the colour green, and the sight of it stirred a memory she had been trying to avoid. Why had she married Sam?

She liked Sam well enough, but the truth had become unavoidable. Shortly after repeating those vows, Evelyn realized she didn't love him.

Sam Greene was thirty-two when she met him. At first, he seemed perfect—he had the right job, the right family background. He was, as her mother put it, "every girl's dream." But after they tied the knot, Evelyn had to face reality. Sam was boring. He was a snob, the kind of man who cared more about appearances than authenticity.

Evelyn often thought she'd have been happier married to someone completely different. A construction worker, maybe. Just a good man who loved her for who she was.

Monica was more than a friend—she was Evelyn's confidante. An artist who lived unapologetically, Monica didn't care what the world thought of her. Evelyn often envied that about her. Monica knew exactly what she wanted, while Evelyn felt she was still figuring it out.

She turned to study her reflection in the mirror. The dress hugged her curves perfectly, accentuating the curves of her hips and the fullness of her breasts. She liked the confidence she felt, and how powerful it made her.

Evelyn had spent over an hour straightening the kinks in her hair with a flat iron, smoothing it into dark brown tresses that cascaded beyond her shoulders. Her full lips—a striking feature she inherited from her African mother, were glossy. Her father, an Italian, had passed down her caramel complexion and elegant bone structure.

As a young girl, Evelyn had done a bit of modelling, though it was more her mother's connections than her passion that opened those doors. And it was those connections that had secured her a job as an executive assistant—a position she appreciated, but it wasn't her dream job.

CLUTCHING THE LARGE VELVET BOX AGAINST HER BODY, EVELYN EXITED THE lobby of her building. It was mid-June, and the night was warm. As she walked away from her building, she took deep breaths to calm her nerves.

Personal effects were prohibited, so Evelyn wore no jewelry— not even her wedding ring. She had slipped her driver's license into the pocket of her silk dress.

The walk to the pickup location was easy because Evelyn was wearing flats. The moment she arrived, a black-tinted Tesla pulled up next to her. Startled, she felt the vehicle had followed her since she left her building.

The gull wing door opened upwards, and as she entered the vehicle, she gasped, shocked to find she was alone. There was no driver. After placing the black box on the seat beside her, Evelyn loosened the ribbon she had tried to tie the same way it had arrived. She had failed to replicate the perfect presentation from before.

Somewhat terrified of the absence of a driver, Evelyn closed her eyes. Yet, something was fulfilling about the fear she felt—something exciting.

"Welcome. Please complete the next step," a voice echoed from the speakers within the car.

Evelyn knew what she needed to do. She had read the instructions.

2

Clayton Muttler sat at the edge of his bed, staring at the wooden floor beneath his size 12 feet. Today marked the first anniversary of his mother's death, and he still couldn't believe she was gone. Mona Muttler had passed away at just forty-four years old. Losing her so young was difficult enough, but for it to happen the day before Clayton's twenty-ninth birthday had shattered him.

He sighed, feeling a heavy weight of grief in his chest. Birthdays would never feel the same again. Turning thirty tomorrow was not something he could look forward to; it felt hollow without her.

Mona had loved him with the fierce devotion of a single mother who had given everything for her child. For as long as he could remember, it had been Mona and "Little Clay." However, when he turned twelve, his mother's friends had dropped the "Little." At 6-foot-five, he was anything but small—a trait he knew had come from his father's side of the family.

The thought of the man he'd never met stirred a confusing mix of anger and curiosity. Clayton knew who his father was now—he had learned his identity on the day of his mother's funeral. The man had no idea that Clayton even existed.

Almost a year had passed since that revelation, and Clayton still hadn't found the courage to confront him. After what he had discovered, Clayton knew the day would come when he would look that man in the eyes and ask him some questions.

After a quick shower and large cup of coffee, Clayton left the little bungalow he'd bought a few months after becoming a constable. Those early years as a rookie were tough, but Clayton felt proud after finally making detective.

Clayton had been partnered with a seasoned detective, Rodney Johnson, who was the biggest know-it-all he'd ever met. Clayton smirked at the thought as he climbed into his black Range Rover. Johnson, a man in his forties, had an air of authority that made it hard to argue with him. For a brief moment, Clayton swore he could hear his mother's voice in his head, gently reminding him to respect his elders.

With a sigh, Clayton started the engine and drove toward his first destination. He pressed the accelerator harder than usual—he was already five minutes late. His aunt didn't like waiting, not even for her favourite nephew.

Ruby Chambers was the epitome of a strong Black woman. Though she and Clayton were not blood-related, she would always be his Aunt Ruby. At forty-five, she looked more like Clayton's older sister than his aunt.

Ruby and Mona Muttler had been best friends, as close as sisters. As

Clayton entered the cemetery, he spotted Ruby standing by his mother's grave. She was hard to miss, even from a distance.

"Come on, boy! I ain't got all day to wait in this place," she called out, her voice carrying across the quiet cemetery. Then, as if catching herself, she turned to the tombstone and softened. "Sorry, girl."

Ruby hated cemeteries. A deeply superstitious woman, she believed the living shouldn't spend too much time among the dead.

Clayton reached her side, kissed her cheek, and stepped back to take her in. "You're looking fine as always, Aunt Ruby."

"And why not fine, huh? You expect me to come out here looking horrible?" She gestured at her outfit—a sharp, modern outfit that looked like it had come straight from the latest fashion catalogue.

Clayton blinked back the sting of tears. The sight of her brought back memories of his mother. Ruby and Mona had been alike in so many ways.

Ruby must have noticed the shift in his expression because she quickly changed the subject. "Look at you, all handsome with that detective badge on your belt. And boy, it seems you ain't stopped growing yet neither."

"At six foot five, Aunt Ruby, I think I'm done growing," Clayton replied with a grin.

"You keep looking like that, and you're gonna make me cry." Ruby turned back toward the marble tombstone, her voice thick with emotion. "Mona would be proud of you, you know that?"

Clayton stepped closer to her as they both stared at the grave. For a moment, neither of them spoke. The silence was heavy but not unwelcome—it felt like Mona was there with them.

As he walked her to her car, Clayton had a feeling he knew what his aunt was about to say. Sure enough, the words came as if she'd been holding them in all morning.

"It's been a year, Clay. When are you planning on seeing your father?"

"Ain't no reason for me to see him, is there?"

Aunt Ruby stopped and took his hand, her tone soft but firm. "Child, you know it's what your mama wanted."

Clayton's jaw tightened. He couldn't recall a single time in his life when he'd been angry at his mother—except the day of her funeral. That was when Aunt Ruby handed him the envelope. He didn't open it until hours later, and when he read the contents, fury bubbled up like never before.

"Now, tell me, Aunt Ruby," he said, his voice low, "why should I have anything to do with that man?" His thoughts flicked to the letter—his mother's letter—locked away in the safe at home. It was too painful to reread, but he could never bring himself to throw it away.

Ruby sighed, her gaze steady. "Because he's your father. And in your line of work, he can do things for you—help you, move you up in the world." She paused, her eyes searching his. "It's the least he can do."

Clayton shook his head, the anger simmering just beneath the surface. "Not gonna happen. Not after what he did."

3

Clayton's phone rang, and he welcomed the interruption when Johnson's name flashed on the screen. Quickly kissing Aunt Ruby's cheek, he lifted the phone. "Gotta go, Aunt Ruby. It's work."

He hurried away, pressing the phone to his ear.

"You be careful out there now," Aunt Ruby called after him.

Before Johnson could speak, Clayton gave his aunt a thumbs-up without looking back. "Yeah."

"What's the deal, Muttler?" Johnson's voice cut through, sharp and impatient. "Dawson was pissed, man! What the hell are you trying to do, make me look bad? We were supposed to meet him an hour ago."

Clayton climbed into his car, shutting the door with a solid thud. He started the engine, his stomach sinking. "Shit, man... I'm sorry. It's my mother's—"

"Save it, kid." Johnson's tone softened just enough to show a flicker of understanding, though it was clear he wasn't in the mood for emotional conversations. "Don't worry about it. One day, you'll have to cover my ass."

"You bet."

"Good. Now get your ass to 13 Watt Avenue right away! And bring coffee—you're gonna fucking need it today. It's our first homicide together, kid. Let's not screw it up."

"I'm on my way," Clay said.

Rodney Johnson replied with a barely audible grunt before adding his last words, "And bring three coffees. Dawson is waiting for us on-site, and the least you can do is bring something to cheer him up."

Clay could feel his heart race. "Dawson's at the scene? Sounds like a big one."

Johnson sighed, clearly frustrated. "That still doesn't explain why the hell he needs to be there."

His partner abruptly ended the call. Clay had heard the rumours—office gossip about how Dawson and Johnson could barely be in the same room without clashing.

---

13 WATT AVENUE WAS AN ABANDONED HERITAGE BUILDING, AND AS CLAYTON stepped out of his vehicle and approached Johnson, it was obvious this was a dump site.

The old brick building was vacant. Graffiti covered the walls, and although it was daylight, the red and blue lights from the police cruisers strobed over the brick pavement in the alley.

Sergeant Wade Dawson, Clayton's boss, strode toward them as soon as he reached Johnson. The portly man immediately helped himself to one of the three large coffees Clayton had brought and took a long gulp before speaking. Clayton nodded, trying to hide his reaction, but it was too late—Dawson's tie hung loose around his neck, looking like it might be as old as Clayton himself.

Clayton offered up a small white box. "Craig's Cookies," he said. "Had to wait in line for these." He glanced at Johnson, silently pleading for his new partner to chime in and explain why he was late. But Johnson clutched his coffee in his oversized hand, sipping casually as if nothing were wrong.

Dawson popped open the box and grabbed one of the chunky cookies. "You trying to make me fatter than I already am, Muttler?"

Clayton blinked, uncertain how to respond.

The sergeant bit into the cookie, his eyebrows shooting up as he chewed. "Not bad at all, kid."

Wade Dawson wasn't a tall man, but his confidence more than made up for his lack of stature. The silver at his temples gave him a distinguished air, and his thick hair was slicked into place with what was probably too much product.

SHE WAS IN HER LATE TWENTIES, WITH DARK HAIR AND STRIKING CHEEKBONES. Clayton stood between his boss and his partner, gazing at the naked woman. Her skin was dark, and her full lips were slightly parted, as though she were posing for a photographer. But she was dead. Her pristine body was propped up, its back resting against a brick wall. Clayton watched as Dawson knelt in front of her.

"Who the hell could do something like this?" Dawson muttered, not touching the corpse—no one could do that until forensics arrived.

"Tell me what you see, Clay," Johnson said, crossing his arms over his broad chest. "Give me your thoughts on this one."

As Clayton studied the area around the body, he tugged at his goatee. "She didn't die here," he said. He crouched beside Dawson, eyeing the woman's fingers. "Nails are nicely painted. She's got nothing on her... no jewelry, no clothes. I think she was dropped off. We've got ourselves a Jane Doe."

Without looking up, Dawson asked, "Not bad, but what else do you see?"

"Uh... there are no wounds or bruises anywhere from what I can tell."

Dawson nodded. "And what about the fact that she might have a husband?"

Clayton furrowed his brows. "Husband?"

"Look at the left hand, kid," Johnson grunted, pausing to pull a Bic pen from his jacket pocket. He pointed toward the victim's ring finger. "Looks like she usually wore a wedding band."

Johnson turned his gaze to Clayton, a smirk playing on his lips. "This girl's as pretty as you are, kid."

Clayton bristled internally, knowing exactly what Johnson meant. The victim was biracial. Clayton, too, had inherited his mixed features—dark skin from his Black father and sharp, angular traits from his Asian mother. Though he knew who his father was, he had no desire to meet the man who had given him his six-foot-five frame but little else.

He realized he'd missed part of what Johnson was saying, and his fists clenched as he forced himself to shake off the distraction. He needed to focus on the case, not the ghost of a man with no place in his life.

"We're dealing with a strategic son of a bitch here," Johnson said, his tone sharp. "She looks too clean—too perfect to be dumped in a place like this."

Dawson nodded in agreement, crossing his arms. "I'd bet a box of those Craig's Cookies that the COD is strangulation." He licked his lips, as if still savouring the decadent treat. "Where's that damn ME? Come on, people! I don't plan on staying here all day!"

Clayton turned at the sound of hurried footsteps approaching. Dawson and Johnson straightened as a figure came into view.

"About fucking time, Chamney!" Johnson called out, motioning toward Clayton with his Bic pen still in hand. "Meet the new kid on the block. Muttler, this here is the worst CSI in the world—Lyle Chamney."

Chamney didn't so much as flinch at the jab. The CSI, wearing snug, powder-free nitrile gloves, glanced at Clayton and offered a faint nod. He was a man in his late forties, his white face framed by blonde cornrow braids that cascaded down his back.

4

Back at the precinct, Clayton did his best to get comfortable in the chair across from Dawson's desk. His palms rested on his knees as he sat stiffly, his unease heightened by Johnson seated next to him, relaxed as ever.

Lyle Chamney, the CSI, had finished examining the area around the body, taking photos and sketching diagrams. Protocol dictated that neither the detectives nor Chamney could touch the body until the medical examiner arrived and completed their work.

Dawson leaned back in his chair, tugging at his tie before tapping the file on his desk with a thick finger. "Based on what we saw and what the ME confirmed, this girl was strangled." He shook his head, his expression a mix of weariness and frustration. "But this guy... this guy must be a real piece of work."

Johnson leaned forward as if to grab the file, but Dawson's sharp glare stopped him mid-motion. Clayton observed the subtle exchange, noting a strange tension between the two men. There was an unspoken challenge in their body language, but he stayed quiet, waiting for his moment.

"Why the hell would someone strangle a woman and then cover the bruises with makeup?" Johnson asked, his tone incredulous. "That's some messed-up shit. I'm betting only a guy would pull a stunt like that."

Clayton finally spoke, his voice measured. "He's a perfectionist."

Dawson's brows rose at the comment, his eyes locked with Clayton's, appraising him. "Go on."

Clayton hesitated for a moment, but it was a relief to let the thoughts escape his mind. "Well... there was a case I read about—something from the 1950s—"

"Oh, give me a fucking break!" Johnson interrupted, his voice laced with frustration. He turned to Dawson, anger flaring in his eyes. "Are you seriously gonna sit there and listen to this crap?"

Dawson shrugged, unfazed. "Let's hear it, Muttler. Tell me what you've got."

Clayton took a breath, unsure if he should continue, but he pushed through. "The marks on Jane Doe's neck—they were precise. Neat, almost like he took his time placing whatever he used to strangle her. It's as if he cared about the process, like it was deliberate. He wasn't in a rush. I think he felt completely in control, like he had all the time in the world to do what he needed to do. Then he brought her to that building and left her there, intentionally."

For a moment, there was silence. Then Dawson nodded, a glint of approval in his expression. "I think you're on to something there, Muttler. I like the way you think."

Clayton's heart slammed against his ribcage as Dawson turned his gaze toward Johnson. The next words left Dawson's mouth with finality. "Johnson, I want you to let Muttler take the lead on this one."

Clayton froze, a mix of elation and dread swelling in his chest. This was the kind of case that could either make his career or shatter it completely. He opened his mouth to respond, but no words came out.

"You want to give a case like this to a rookie?" Johnson snapped. His voice was harsh, dripping with disbelief. "The kid's still wet behind the ears! Hell, he's probably still got his mother's milk in his mouth.

Clayton's expression darkened, and his voice came out cold and sharp. "My mother is dead."

Johnson didn't apologize, his tone curt. "All right, kid. Go on about that case you mentioned."

Clayton cleared his throat, gathering his thoughts. "The guy strangled his victims with pantyhose. Always the same method, same meticulous setup. I think our unsub used something specific to strangle this vic too, and he's gone out of his way to make sure she can't be ID'd. This guy isn't rushed. He likes having time. He's methodical, maybe even ritualistic."

Johnson gave a reluctant nod, his lips tightening as though he hated to admit it. "Not bad, Muttler. Not bad."

Clayton walked back to his desk, the case file for their first investigation clutched in his hand. Johnson kept pace beside him, and though Clayton wanted to avoid conversation, their desks faced each other. As he sat down, he couldn't avoid meeting his partner's eyes.

He slid the file across the desk to Johnson. "What do you make of the ME's estimate on the time of death?

Johnson dragged the folder toward him, his gaze lingering on Clayton. "Sounds about right. She could've been dead for hours, long enough for our unsub to paint over the bruises."

Something about that phrase clicked in Clayton's mind. "Paint over the bruises..." he echoed.

Johnson raised an eyebrow, smirking. "What the hell are you getting at?"

"The makeup. It was flawless—too perfect, like it wasn't done by hand." Clayton snatched the file back before Johnson could open it. He flipped to the CSI photographs, studying them closely.

Out of the corner of his eye, Clayton noticed Johnson watching him, rocking his chair back and forth in silence. Ignoring the scrutiny, Clayton stood and laid the photos on Johnson's desk. "Look at this. See how even the makeup is? It's an exact match to the rest of her skin."

Johnson sighed, exasperated. "Get to the point, Muttler."

"He used an airbrush," Clayton said, his voice steady with realization. "If he's skilled, he could've done it in under ten minutes."

Johnson nodded slowly, a hint of approval in his expression.

Clayton's desk phone rang, and he snatched it up mid-ring. "Detective Muttler," he said, sinking into his chair with a hint of pride.

"Howdy, Clay! I hear you're the lead on this Jane Doe case. Sorry I couldn't shake your hand earlier—it's Lyle."

Clayton raised his eyebrows at Johnson and hit the speakerphone button, cradling the receiver. "Not a problem, Lyle. Johnson and I are here going over your photos. I was just about to call you, man."

"Gracious me, no wonder my ears were ringing!" Lyle Chamney's cheerful tone filled the room. From the moment they'd met, Clayton had liked the guy's easygoing demeanour. "Anyway, you two better skedaddle down here. Found something I think you'll want to see."

"Go grab a coffee, Chamney," Johnson said dryly. "We'll be there in half an hour."

Clayton hung up, turning to Johnson, who rolled his eyes dramatically.

"Sounds like Chamney knows his stuff," Clayton said.

"He's one of the best," Johnson admitted with a groan. "But the guy gets on my last nerve."

Clayton chuckled. "Seems like a nice enough guy to me."

Johnson shook his head. "Wait 'til you see him driving off in that ancient 1991 Saab 900. You'll get it."

5

Clayton followed Johnson into the crime lab, where they found Chamney working diligently at his desk. The soft tones of a Pink Floyd song floated from a small radio, adding a mellow backdrop to the sterile atmosphere. Clayton couldn't see anything remotely annoying about the man and returned Chamney's beaming smile without hesitation.

Chamney's desk was impeccably organized, every item perfectly in its place. As he stepped around it and extended a hand, Clayton shook it firmly. "Nice to finally meet you, Lyle," Clayton said. "Johnson and I were looking at your photos from the scene—we've got a hunch."

Chamney's eyes sparkled with interest. "Do tell."

Johnson sighed loudly, his impatience obvious. "I thought you said you had something we needed to see, Chamney."

Chamney smirked as he lowered himself into his chair. "Never let this job change who you are, Clay," he said, his voice light but earnest. "First piece of advice for you." He turned to Johnson with a playful grin. "Obviously, not everyone takes that to heart."

Clayton stifled a laugh, but his grin gave him away. "Alright, Lyle, what've you got for us?"

Chamney handed a sealed evidence bag to Clayton, who stared at it, perplexed. The bag seemed empty. Chamney grinned. "Look carefully, my friend. I know it seems like there's nothing there, but what you're holding is the only piece of physical evidence... well, aside from the body."

Johnson snatched the bag from Clayton's hand, holding it up to the light. "What is this?"

"It's hard to see with the naked eye," Chamney said, leaning back in his chair. "But nothing escapes yours truly—not under my lights and microscope."

Johnson hissed, shaking his head in annoyance.

"What is it?" Clayton asked, leaning closer. At first glance, he thought the tiny object was just a strand of the victim's hair.

"Raw silk," Chamney said, his voice light but confident. "Nestled in her hair, right at the nape of her neck."

Clayton glanced at Johnson, who was already staring at him intently. Their eyes met, and Clayton voiced the thought forming between them. "Do you think he could have used silk to strangle her?"

Chamney shrugged, flicking a long braid over his shoulder as he grinned. "Good gracious! You expect me to find all the answers, Clay? I just give you what I find... but, yeah, some killers do have their preferred methods or tools."

Johnson interjected, clearly eager to move things along. "Muttler thinks our unsub might've used something specific to kill this girl—like maybe he's got a pantyhose fetish or some other kink."

Chamney nodded thoughtfully. "I see where you're going with this."

Clayton glanced toward the door, then back at Chamney. "Maybe we should take another look at the body," he said. "We also think the killer may have used an airbrush to cover the bruises—it was too perfect to be done by hand."

Chamney's eyes lit up with admiration as he studied Clayton. "Good heavens, aren't you the clever one." His gaze lingered. "Rodney, maybe you two should check the body again. I'm sure young Mr. Holmes here will spot something we missed."

Without a word, Johnson turned and walked toward the door, his impatience obvious.

ANONYME

Clayton had not expected the morgue to feel so cold. There was a chill that seeped through his blazer and into his bones. He could hear the faint buzz of the overhead fluorescent lights, and their harsh glow bleaching every surface in sterile white and pale grey. The stainless steel countertops gleamed under the light.

Clayton gazed at the row of refrigeration units lining one wall. The doors were identical save for the small labels affixed to them. The room was silent, save for the soft hum of the ventilation system and the occasional metallic clink of instruments being set down by the pathologist.

Wondering if he looked out of place, Clayton glanced at his partner. Johnson seemed at ease, already standing over the body, his posture steady and unflinching. "Let's get this over with," Johnson said, his tone firm as he peeled back the white sheet.

The victim's neck was exposed, and the bruises, now free of the makeup that had concealed them, stood out sharply against her brown skin. Clayton leaned in closer, careful not to touch the body.

The girl's face drew his attention, and for a moment, a wave of sadness crashed over him. Her features, lifeless and serene, stirred memories he had long tried to suppress—his mother's face filled his mind. Clayton tightened his jaw, forcing himself to push the thoughts away and focus.

"These marks," he said, his voice steady but low, "definitely came from some kind of noose or soft object."

"Like raw silk," Johnson agreed, his eyes locked on the evidence as he straightened.

"Why do you suppose he left her naked and perfectly posed at the site of an abandoned historic building?" Clayton asked, keeping his gaze fixed on the victim's face, searching for answers in her lifeless features.

"Dunno," Johnson muttered, his eyes narrowing as he thought it through. "But if your airbrush theory is right, there might be something to why he wanted her found there." He paused, turning to meet Clayton's gaze. "You think this was done by a man?"

Clayton didn't hesitate. "I doubt a woman would spend so much time making another woman look... so perfect."

Clayton turned to the pathologist, who had been silent since allowing them access to the body. "It's Sophia, right?"

"Ever since I could remember," she replied with a faint smile, flicking her brown hair out of her eyes.

"What can you tell us about silk? Specifically, if it were used as a garrote to strangle someone." Clayton gestured toward the body. "That silk fibre found in her hair—could it have been placed there deliberately?"

Sophia crossed her arms thoughtfully. "I'd say yes... but only if the killer enjoys playing games."

Johnson stepped closer, his expression skeptical. "Could he really have used silk as a weapon?"

Sophia pointed to the victim's neck, her tone confident and clinical. "Based on the width and pattern of the ligature marks, it's possible. See here? The marks are too wide for wire or cord. Raw silk is more elastic, though—it would make strangulation harder to control, requiring significant strength and precision."

Clayton nodded, processing her words. "So he's strong. He's got an ego. But using silk... it tells me he's either sophisticated or wants people to think he is."

Sophia eyed the body again, her expression softening as she shook her head. "Poor girl," she murmured.

Clayton took a step toward the door, his gaze fixed forward, avoiding another glance at the lifeless form on the table. "Thanks for your help, Sophia," he said, his tone steady but edged with determination. "We need to get an ID on her. Knowing who she is will bring us closer to finding who did this to her."

6

Clayton woke early the next morning, the restless night leaving him groggy and heavy-eyed. It was his birthday. Turning thirty didn't feel much different from twenty-five. His thoughts, as they often did, wandered to his mother. These days, he couldn't think of himself without thinking of her.

The night before, he had come home late after poring over the scant details they had on the unidentified victim. Two days dead, and yet no one had reported her missing. The thought gnawed at him, a reminder of how some lives seemed to slip through the cracks.

Johnson had stayed behind at the precinct, tirelessly combing through the CCTV footage from the area. That was the kind of partner he was—relentless, dependable. But as Clayton thought about it, he couldn't shake the nagging question: did Johnson resent him for getting the lead on the case?

Clayton dragged himself to the shower, still sleepy. It was barely six in the morning, but early starts were second nature now. He had a case to solve, and the clock was already ticking.

He slipped into a blue dress shirt and a pair of black Levi's, opting for a casual look that matched his mood. As he stepped outside and headed for his Range Rover, the chill of the early morning air brought his thoughts back to the victim. She was the reason he was doing this—the only reason.

He found Johnson sitting at his desk with the case file in front of him, and from the frustrated look on his face, Clayton could sense they were nowhere closer to getting a lead on the case than they were the previous day.

"Any luck with the CCTV?" Clayton asked, even though he already knew the answer. It was the easiest way to ease into a conversation this early in the day.

Johnson tapped his fingers on the stack of papers in front of him, then rubbed his tired eyes. "I went through footage from every damn camera in the area," he said, his voice heavy with frustration. "How the hell could he have gotten her into that alley without being caught on camera? It doesn't make sense!"

Clayton shrugged. "We think we know how he killed her, and we know he covered the ligature marks around her neck. What we don't know is why he went to such lengths to hide those bruises." He moved behind Johnson's chair, leaning slightly over. "Maybe we should walk the crime scene together," he suggested.

"Yeah," Johnson muttered, running a hand through his hair. "But without knowing who this girl is, we're dead in the water, kid."

"Maybe it'll help us figure out how someone with a dead body managed to dodge all those cameras." Clayton scratched his goatee, his thoughts drifting to who their unsub could be. "This guy must know the area like the back of his hand."

"That doesn't matter." Johnson took a long gulp of his coffee, his tone unwavering. "Everyone makes mistakes. Every killer can be caught." He opened his mouth to add more, but the sharp ring of his desk phone cut him off.

"Yeah!" Johnson barked, snatching the receiver so quickly he nearly dropped it. His eyes seemed to light up with interest. "You're fucking kidding! We're on our way."

Clayton, mid-step toward his own desk, froze by his chair and turned to his partner, his curiosity sharp. "What's going on?"

"That was Winters at the front desk," Johnson said, already striding toward the elevator with purpose. "Someone just came in to report a missing person."

Clayton grabbed his cell phone and hurried after him, his pulse quickening. Something in his gut told him this could be their first real lead in the case.

7

Monica Sinclair sat near the front desk, her cell phone clutched tightly in her hands. She'd called Evie's number several times that morning, each attempt met with silence. No answer, no return call, nothing. She told herself that Sam must have returned home, and Evie was simply busy. But deep down, the gnawing worry wouldn't leave her. Her best friend hadn't even responded to her texts.

She looked up to see two men walking toward her, and Monica instantly knew they were detectives. The older white man had a somewhat shabby appearance—wrinkled shirt, scuffed shoes—but his sharp eyes missed nothing. The taller Black man, however, exuded an effortless confidence that made Monica wish she'd put more thought into what she was wearing that morning.

Quickly, she tucked her cell phone into her pocket and rubbed her palms together nervously.

The officer at the front desk gestured toward her after a brief exchange with the men.

"Miss Sinclair?" The older man shoved his hands into his pockets and gave her a hard, assessing look.

Monica nodded, unable to find her voice in the moment.

"I'm Detective Muttler," said the tall one, his voice calm and reassuring. He offered a slight smile that made her face flush with warmth. "And this is Detective Johnson."

"If you'd come with us, Miss Sinclair," Muttler continued, "we can talk about your friend."

Monica swallowed hard and nodded again. "Uhm... it's just Monica," she said softly.

THE GIRL SAT AT A TABLE ACROSS FROM CLAYTON AND JOHNSON, HER HANDS gripping the glass of water he'd offered. Monica Sinclair took small, tentative sips, her gaze locked on Clayton's. "You think Evie's dead?"

"What we're saying, Miss Sinclair," Johnson interjected, his tone sharp as he tilted his head slightly to the right, "is that the unidentified victim could be Evelyn Greene." The shift in his posture seemed deliberate, as though he wanted to unsettle her.

Clayton shot Johnson a reproachful glance. This wasn't the time for heavy-handed tactics. They needed Monica's full cooperation, not her fear. "What my partner means, Monica, is that we need your help identifying the body we found yesterday. Can you help us with that?"

Monica nodded slowly, her fingers tightening around the glass.

Clayton reached for the folder next to him, pausing for a moment. "I think it's better to show you a photo—no need to take you all the way downstairs." His voice softened, trying to prepare her for what was to come.

Clayton removed the photo from the folder and slid it across the table. Monica's reaction was immediate—her eyes widened with shock, and a sharp gasp escaped her painted red lips.

"Oh my God!" Her voice trembled as she pushed the glass of water aside, nearly spilling it. She reached for the photo, but her hands hesitated mid-air before retreating to her lap. "It's Evie," she whispered.

Clayton nodded solemnly, slipping the photo back into the folder with practiced care. "Thank you, Monica. I'm truly sorry for your loss." His tone was gentle but firm, aiming to steady her. He gestured slightly toward Johnson, who was watching silently. "Rodney and I are going to need your help. We need to know more about your friend—her life, her habits, anything that might help us."

He leaned forward, meeting her tear-filled gaze. "Someone took Evelyn's life, and we won't stop until we bring them to justice."

After spending over an hour with Monica, Clayton found himself frustrated. From what she had shared, Evelyn Greene seemed to have led an ordinary life. Married for two years, living in a quiet neighbourhood, with her husband away on a business trip—it all sounded so mundane, so unremarkable. Why would anyone want her dead?

Clayton glanced at Johnson, who had been watching Monica with a penetrating stare, his chin tucked into his chest, his eyes sharp and unrelenting. Clayton couldn't figure out what his partner was doing, but the intensity of it was beginning to unsettle Monica.

"Johnson, can I have a moment?" Clayton asked, rising from his chair. He didn't wait for a response before heading for the door.

Johnson joined him, his chair scraping loudly as he stood. Outside the room, Clayton turned to face him, lowering his voice but keeping it firm. "What are you trying to do in there? Scare her off?"

"No, kid," Johnson replied, his tone unapologetic, arms crossed. "I'm digging for the truth—the real truth."

Clayton frowned. "What're you talking about?"

Johnson pointed back toward the interrogation room. "That girl in there? She's hiding something. I'm sure of it. And whatever she's holding back is the key to this case."

Clayton opened his mouth to respond, but Johnson raised a hand, cutting him off. His voice softened but carried weight. "No, Muttler. This time, you listen to me. You can go running to Dawson if you want, but I'm telling you, I've seen this before. She knows something, and it's written all over her face."

Clayton's jaw tightened as Johnson stepped closer, his hand resting firmly on Clayton's shoulder. "Look, I know you're the golden boy around here. You're tall, polished, and Dawson thinks you can do no wrong. But I've been doing this a hell of a lot longer, and my gut says she's not telling us everything. Trust me on this one, kid."

Clayton exhaled sharply and moved toward the door without another word. Dawson had handed him the lead on this case, but Johnson was right about one thing—experience counted for something. If his partner had a gut feeling, Clayton needed to let it run its course.

Before opening the door, Clayton glanced back at Johnson. "You think she'll crack if you press her?"

Johnson smirked. "They always do. Trust me, kid."

Clayton nodded once, his jaw tight. "Just... don't push her too far. We need her cooperation."

Johnson's smirk softened into something more serious. "I know where to draw the line, Muttler. Let me do my thing."

Without replying, Clayton opened the door and stepped back inside.

8

Johnson's plan worked. As Monica spoke, Clayton discreetly used the Evernote app to jot down notes while the Voice Memo app on his phone recorded every word.

Monica's hands were clasped tightly in her lap, her knuckles white. "I... I didn't think it'd matter. Evie... she was a very private person, and she didn't expect me to tell anyone this." Her voice wavered as she looked down, guilt flickering in her eyes.

"This is no betrayal, Monica," Clayton said, his tone calm but firm. "You're helping us catch Evelyn's killer. Anything you know could make a difference."

Monica pursed her lips, hesitating. "Sam... her husband... well, Evie knew he was going away, and..." She faltered, her voice dropping to a whisper. "All of this—it's my fault."

Johnson leaned forward, his elbows resting on the table, his tone sharp but not unkind. "What about her husband, Monica?"

Monica looked up at him, her eyes glistening. "Evie wasn't happy. Sam was always working, always traveling. She realized she didn't really love him anymore—maybe she never did." She paused, wiping her eyes quickly.

Clayton and Johnson exchanged a glance but said nothing, giving her the space to continue.

"On the surface, Sam seems like a nice guy. But underneath? He's a real snob." Monica's lip curled into a sneer. "You know the type—golf on weekends, luxury trips, expensive suits. Always about appearances."

Clayton highlighted Samuel Greene's name in his notes, underlining it as a potential suspect. "What about Sam's family?" he asked gently.

Monica shrugged, her expression wary. "I didn't know them. I barely talked to Sam when I saw him—just the usual polite stuff. But his family? They're well-off. They never approved of him marrying Evie... especially not so young."

"They didn't approve of Evelyn?" Johnson asked, frowning.

"No," Monica said, shaking her head. "None of them came to the wedding. They made it pretty clear they didn't think she was good enough for him. Sam has four sisters. He's the only son."

Clayton hadn't forgotten Monica's earlier words. "You said it was your fault. Why is that?"

Monica hesitated, her expression shifting to one of embarrassment. Her glare shifted to Johnson as she spoke. "I know you'll judge her... and me for this. After all, you're men. But why is it women have to play by different rules? Why shouldn't we take control of our own lives?"

Clayton tilted his head, his voice calm. "I'm not sure I follow, Monica."

"Like I said before, Evie wasn't happy. She was a nice girl. Any guy would want her." Monica's tone grew sharper as her gaze flickered between the two detectives. "We... Evie and I... were sure Sam was seeing another woman. I mean, they barely did anything together—you know, sex?"

"Go on," Johnson said, his voice even but his eyes narrowing slightly.

Monica glanced away before continuing. "One evening, Evie and I went for a walk downtown, and we passed this massive billboard—you know, the one right in the square?"

Clayton noted the impatient look on Johnson's face but kept his focus on Monica. "I know the one," Clayton said.

"It was an ad for that posh service, Anonyme." Monica leaned forward slightly, her voice lowering as though revealing a secret. "You know what I'm talking about, right?"

Clayton and Johnson exchanged a glance, neither answering immediately.

"It's a dating service," Monica continued, exasperated. "But not just any dating service—it's for married people looking to cheat. I guess singles use it too. It's all over the city." She frowned deeply, her voice trembling. "Evie and I thought Sam was doing his own thing, so we decided to use the service. She was nervous about it, so I signed up and went first..."

Clayton felt his pulse quicken. He exchanged a glance with Johnson, who raised an eyebrow, clearly skeptical but intrigued.

"You signed up?" Johnson leaned forward slightly, folding his arms across his chest.

Monica nodded, her cheeks flushing. "I thought it was harmless at first. You know, just to check... to see if Evie would want to create a profile."

"And?" Clayton prompted gently, trying to keep her talking.

Monica leaned forward, her voice lowering as if sharing a forbidden secret. "It's not just about the sex. It's the exclusivity—the secrecy. You're paying for discretion, for control, and for the thrill of not knowing. For some people, that's worth any price." She hesitated, glancing between the two detectives. "And... let's be real. The people who can afford it? They're not exactly the type who'd settle for a hookup app."

Clayton rubbed his temple, processing the absurdity of it all. "So, you're saying Evelyn signed up for this? She paid five thousand dollars to sleep with a stranger?"

Monica looked pained. "We both did. I told her I'd do it first, to see how it worked. I thought it'd be fun, you know? Just harmless fun. But then she got curious and said she wanted to try it, too."

"Did she go through with it?" Johnson asked, his tone sharpening.

"Yes." Monica's voice wavered. "She was a bit nervous, but she seemed... happier, curious, like she wanted to do something she'd been missing."

"And when was this?" Clayton asked, still taking notes.

"The day before she disappeared," Monica whispered.

Johnson straightened, the tension in his posture obvious. "And you didn't think to mention this earlier?"

"I didn't know it mattered!" Monica snapped, tears brimming in her eyes. "I didn't know she'd end up dead!"

Clayton held up a hand to calm her. "We're not blaming you, Monica. But this is important. Do you have any receipts, emails, anything from this service that might help us trace her steps?"

Monica shook her head. "It's all designed to leave no trail. No emails, no receipts with names—just an encrypted portal. They even use private drivers to pick you up and take you to the... appointment."

Clayton and Johnson exchanged glances.

"This service—Anonyme—it sounds like a breeding ground for people with money and secrets," Clayton said, his voice low.

"And maybe for predators," Johnson added grimly. "We need to find out where this 'appointment' happened and who Evelyn met that night."

Monica looked down at her hands. "I can show you the site," she offered. "But you won't find much. They're good at hiding things."

"Let us worry about that," Clayton said, his tone resolute. "If there's a way in, we'll find it."

9

Monica Sinclair had been talking for nearly three hours, her voice growing increasingly steady with each passing minute. Clayton knew their next step would be to interview Evelyn Greene's husband, but there was still something in Monica's words that kept him anchored to the moment. He glanced at Johnson, who was immersed in preparing subpoenas for Evelyn and Sam Greene's financial records, the sound of typing filling the room. But Monica wasn't finished yet—her story still held gaps, and Clayton had questions that needed answers.

"You mentioned earlier that Evelyn wasn't happy. Did she and Sam argue often?" Clayton asked, glancing over his shoulder after hearing Johnson's grunt in response.

Monica shook her head, taking a long sip of water before answering. "No, it wasn't like that. Sam's a quiet guy. Evelyn, on the other hand, always said what was on her mind. But Sam? He never spoke his thoughts. The guy... he freaked me out."

From across the room, Johnson's voice floated over. "Sounds like a recipe for trouble. Silent types are always the hardest to read." He didn't look up from his laptop, his fingers still tapping the keys.

Clayton kept his focus on Monica, though he couldn't help but agree with Johnson. "Why did Evelyn think Sam was having an affair?"

Monica didn't hesitate, the words spilling out with a bitterness that suggested deeper feelings of resentment toward her friend's husband. "Sam's just a strange guy. When I visited, he barely said a word, never tried to hang out with us. He was always lurking somewhere nearby or holed up in another room, staring at his phone." She paused, eyes narrowing as if recalling something that still bothered her. "Look, before she was married, Evelyn was two paycheques away from being evicted, and Sam? Sam would have married anyone just to escape his family. He's got a good job, yeah, but if he ever quit, his family's money would always be there to cushion him."

Johnson asked the next question from across the room. "And what did Evelyn do for work?"

Monica smiled faintly. "I used to tell her to just stay home and spend his family's money. All she'd have to do is have a kid, and she'd be set for life." She took another sip of water. "Evie worked as an assistant at the Mayor's office. You know, the one who's always on TV?"

Clayton shot her a quick glance, his eyes briefly leaving the Evernote app on his phone. "The Mayor?"

"Yeah," Monica confirmed, "Evie worked for Elijah Brooks."

Monica shifted in her seat and looked toward the door. "Sorry, but can I be excused for a moment? I really need to use the bathroom."

Clayton nodded and pointed toward the hallway. "It's down the hall, first door on the left."

Monica was gone for several minutes, giving Clayton a chance to get Johnson's opinion on everything they'd learned so far. He walked over to the other table, where Johnson was still focused on the subpoenas.

"What do you make of this so far?" Clayton asked, leaning against the table.

Johnson chuckled. "She's a real piece of work, that one." He shot Clayton a stony glare. "Did you hear her talk about Evelyn getting pregnant and being set for life? What ever happened to women taking control of their own lives, huh?"

Clayton nodded in agreement. "At least Evelyn decided not to take her best friend's advice on that one."

Johnson turned to stare at him. "Hey, why'd you seem spooked about the vic working for Brooks?"

Clayton pivoted nervously. "Nothing. Just seems funny that our vic shares the same boss, that's all." He could see in Johnson's eyes that he didn't believe him.

The door creaked open, and Monica walked back in.

Johnson took the lead on the questioning, clearly eager to wrap up the meeting. "So, this thing, Anonyme. What else can you tell us about it, seeing as you've tried it yourself?"

Monica seemed to ponder for a moment before answering. "Everything's a mystery. Like I said before, once you sign up and pay, they send you a package the next day, and with it, instructions on where to go to get picked up."

Clayton glanced up from his notes, his fingers still hovering over the Evernote app. He caught Johnson's eye across the table. Both of them were eager to finish up the conversation, but the new details kept pulling them in. "What's in the package?"

"We're talking real expensive stuff. It's a huge velvet box left outside your door, and inside, you find the mask you've chosen." Monica said.

Clayton paused, his phone resting on the table now as his gaze sharpened. "Wait, did you say a mask?"

Monica nodded, a small smile tugging at her lips. "Exactly." Her eyes brightened. She leaned forward slightly, animated now. "It's all anonymous, right? You get to choose which mask you want to wear—like a lion, or a cheetah—anything you like. Or it could be the mask of Apollo. You're only allowed to bring one piece of ID, but your phone, your purse, even your jewelry—all that stays at home. You can only wear dark colours—black or blue." She took a deep breath, excitement evident in her voice. "On the day of the appointment, you show up at the rendezvous point where a black-tinted Tesla picks you up. That's when the excitement starts."

Clayton exchanged a quick glance with Johnson. Both of them were processing the bizarre details Monica was revealing.

Johnson shook his head. "A Tesla? And no jewelry? Sounds like a cult, not a night out."

Monica's smile widened, clearly enjoying the reaction. "It's not a cult. It's... well, it's more like an experience." She took another sip of water, seeming to gather her thoughts.

"And these Teslas—are they self-driving?" Clayton asked, his interest piqued.

Monica nodded enthusiastically. "Yep. You get in, and there's no driver. This voice tells you to put on your gear. You have no idea where the car is taking you. You just follow the instructions, and enjoy the ride, wondering where you'll end up."

Clayton raised an eyebrow, leaning forward. "You had no idea where they were taking you?"

Monica eyed him as though his question was almost too simple. "That's the whole point, isn't it? When you get in, you find a VR headset in the back seat. Once you put it on, things change—they control what you see. It's all part of the experience. You're told when to remove the VR headset and put your mask on."

IT WAS NEARLY 7 PM, AND CLAYTON SAT AT HIS DESK, TWIRLING CHINESE noodles onto his chopsticks from a takeout box. Across from him, Johnson slurped down his second serving of wonton soup, looking far too comfortable.

Clayton gestured toward his partner with his chopsticks, chewing quickly before speaking. "Can you believe what she told us?" He scooped up another mouthful of noodles.

Johnson raised an eyebrow as he stabbed at a wonton with his spoon.

"You mean the part about banging some broad you don't know in a secret location while both of you are wearing masks?" He popped the wonton into his mouth, shaking his head in mock disbelief. "You think Dawson would sign off on ten grand for us to check it out—you know, go undercover?"

Clayton nearly choked on his noodles, bowing his head in laughter. "Yeah, I'm sure that'd go over well. Dawson wouldn't approve that, not even for his golden boy."

Johnson smirked. "If he went, what kind of mask do you think he'd pick."

Clayton shook his head, stifling a grin. "Stop. I don't want that mental image while I'm eating."

Johnson brought the bowl to his mouth and gulped the last of his soup noisily. "No, seriously, we gotta find out more about this place. Every business has a head office."

Clayton nodded, setting his chopsticks down for a moment. "Monica said there were about fifty masked men in that place when she went."

"These people must be loaded," Johnson said, shaking his head in disbelief. "Who the hell can afford to throw these parties for over a hundred people in a space where walls open up like magic to join rooms?"

Clayton raised an eyebrow, tapping the side of his takeout box. "Yeah, I almost forgot about that part. Monica said the men and women are kept in separate rooms until one of those walls retracts, joining the two rooms into one." He paused, taking a swig of apple juice to wash down his noodles.

"Sounds like some billionaire's idea of fun," Johnson muttered, leaning back in his chair. "How the hell do you even rent a place like that? Zillow doesn't have a category for secret lairs with retractable walls."

Clayton let out a dry laugh, but his expression turned thoughtful. "It's not just the money, though. The way Monica described it, this thing feels... calculated. Everything from the masks to the VR headsets. Someone's put a lot of thought—and resources—into making sure it all stays anonymous."

Johnson grunted. "Yeah, and that level of control usually means one thing—someone's got something to hide. But you're paying for the *experience*, right? Wasn't that what Monica said?"

The room fell quiet for a moment, save for the occasional scrape of chopsticks or spoon against takeout containers. Both men were processing the layers of secrecy surrounding *Anonyme*.

10

Clayton had spent the entire day at the precinct, and now, exhausted and finally home, he allowed himself a small comfort. Standing by the kitchen counter, he scooped grape nut ice cream into a bowl—his favourite. The simple act gave him a moment to breathe, though his mind was unsettled.

The day's revelations replayed relentlessly in his head. A young woman had been murdered, and he had no idea how long it would take to bring her killer to justice. That weight alone was enough, but there was more. The letter from his late mother lingered at the edge of his thoughts, the one where she'd pleaded with him to reach out to his father—a man he had spent his entire life without.

Clayton sighed and shoved a spoonful of ice cream into his mouth, a perfect distraction. Walking to the couch, he felt the weight of his emotions pressing down harder.

Then there was Evelyn Greene. Her death was tragic enough, but the shock came when he learned where she'd worked: the office of Elijah Brooks.

His father.

The word felt foreign, even in the privacy of his thoughts. Elijah Brooks had no idea Clayton existed, and Clayton wanted to keep it that way. But now, the case might force him to face the man he had spent an entire year avoiding.

For years, Clayton had seen this man—the mayor of his city—on television, giving speeches, shaking hands, and commanding attention. Yet, he hadn't known the truth until the day of his mother's funeral. That was the day her carefully guarded secret unraveled, the day Clayton learned who Elijah Brooks really was.

And Clayton understood why she'd kept it from him. He didn't blame her for the silence, not when the truth carried so much pain and complication. But now, the very case he was working might drag that truth out into the open, whether he was ready for it or not.

Clayton sank into the couch, his ice cream untouched as he stared at the blank television screen. His thoughts were a jumble of fear, anger, and a reluctant sense of duty. The idea of meeting Brooks terrified him, but he couldn't ignore the connection—not when it might be tied to Evelyn's death.

As the ice cream began to melt in the bowl resting on his lap, Clayton leaned back and closed his eyes, trying to steady his racing thoughts.

11

Rodney Johnson left home early, leaving his wife, Lina, puzzled. It wasn't the early start—those were routine—but she couldn't help teasing him about the extra effort he'd put into grooming his hair and donning one of his better suits.

As he parked his sedan in the heart of downtown, Johnson grinned, thinking back to their exchange. Lina had smirked at him over her coffee cup, her curiosity obvious. "What's the occasion?" she'd asked, watching him adjust his tie in the mirror.

He'd kissed her lightly, his hand settling at her slender waist. "I've got a hot date with the Mayor," he said with a playful wink.

Her laughter followed him out the door, and the thought of it still lingered as he stepped onto the bustling sidewalk, ready for whatever the day would bring.

Johnson pulled out his phone, ready to snap a few photos. He'd found exactly what he was looking for.

Standing in the heart of the bustling city square, he gazed up at the massive billboard towering above the crowds of pedestrians and passing cars. Its sheer size and placement made it impossible to miss, but it wasn't just its prominence that caught his attention—it was the ad itself.

The design was simple yet striking, and Johnson couldn't help but silently applaud the brilliance behind the campaign. The clean white background was a perfect canvas for the bold, golden letters spelling out the name: Anonyme.

But what truly captured his gaze were the figures on the billboard.

A woman stood front and centre, draped in a sleek black dress with thin spaghetti straps, one strap slipping seductively off her shoulder. Her pose was alluring, arms crossed over her torso as though guarding a secret, the tilt of her head daring anyone to uncover it. But the real focus was the mask she wore—a masterpiece in itself.

It was Cleopatra. Vibrant colours brought the queen's likeness to life, with intricate designs emphasizing her regal beauty and sensuality.

Behind her, partially blurred as though fading into the white background, stood a male figure. He exuded power even in the haze, his body language predatory yet magnetic. It was as if he were stalking her—or perhaps protecting her. The ambiguity of his presence was intentional, but there was no mistaking his identity.

The mask said it all.

Tutankhamun.

Johnson lowered his phone after taking a few shots, unable to suppress a grin. The mystery was palpable, the allure undeniable. For a brief moment, he wondered if Clayton would think the same thing he was. Johnson knew he'd have one hell of a story to share back at the precinct.

12

Clayton looked up from the paperwork spread before him to find Johnson grinning down at him. His partner's sharp appearance didn't go unnoticed. Clayton took one look at the neatly pressed suit and freshly polished shoes and knew exactly why Johnson had gone the extra mile. They were heading to Evelyn's workplace later that morning.

Clayton sighed, the weight of the impending visit settling heavily on him. It wasn't just the workplace visit—it was the man they'd have to speak with. Elijah Brooks. The city's mayor. His father.

No one knew the truth about their connection, apart from his aunt Ruby and himself. Clayton had gone to great lengths to keep it that way. He avoided meeting Johnson's gaze, instead glancing up at the clock on the wall.

"Did you sleep in, or were you spending all that time getting dressed up for our boss?" he asked, his tone half-teasing but with an edge of distraction.

Johnson's grin widened as he pulled out his phone. "No, kid. I was out doing what I figured you'd have done, given the whole Anonyme thing that girl mentioned." He unlocked his phone and placed it on the desk in front of Clayton.

The screen displayed a photo of a sleek advertisement, its bold design impossible to ignore. Johnson jabbed at the screen. "At five grand a visit, can you imagine the kind of dough this thing rakes in? Look at this ad—simple, classy, and loaded with mystery. I've seen amateur campaigns that cost a fortune, but this? This is another level."

Clayton's brow furrowed as he absorbed the details of the image, questions about Anonyme swirling in his mind—the opulence, the secrecy—but no matter how hard he tried to focus, his thoughts kept veering back to Elijah Brooks and the promise his mother had begged him to keep, even from her grave.

Clayton nodded, still staring at the images on Johnson's phone. "I did plan on checking out that billboard after work." He looked up, offering a faint smile. "Smart thinking, man."

Johnson gave a modest shrug. "What about you? What've you been up to, getting in so early?"

"The phone numbers Monica gave us? The tech team pulled Evelyn's GPS history," Clayton replied, setting the phone aside. "Evelyn's phone pinged near the usual spots—work and home—but there's nothing linking her to this place. Makes sense, considering clients can't bring phones to their appointments." He leaned back in his chair, rubbing his temples in frustration.

"What about Monica Sinclair and the husband?" Johnson asked, leaning forward.

Clayton shuffled through a stack of papers, pulling out a few sheets. "Nothing much on Monica—at least, nothing she didn't already tell us. Tech found some texts between her and Evelyn, just confirming what she said." He paused, holding up two more sheets with a pointed look. "But Samuel Greene is a whole other story."

"GET THIS." CLAYTON PERCHED ON THE EDGE OF HIS DESK, HOLDING UP A sheet of paper. "Turns out our vic's husband, Sam Greene, may have been having an affair."

"Go on," Johnson urged, though his eyes darted to his watch. His body language was tense.

"You in a hurry?" Clayton asked, raising a brow.

"I saw Dawson on the way in," Johnson replied, his tone low.

"Something wrong?"

Johnson shook his head, his expression hard to read. "He wants an update on what we've got so far."

Clayton frowned. "Already? Evelyn Greene was just a regular citizen. Why's he pressing us for a report when we've barely scratched the surface?"

"Good question." Johnson folded his arms, his frustration visible. "But you know Dawson—he doesn't like to wait. You'd think we were solving the mayor's murder the way he's acting."

Clayton smirked at the irony, but it faded as he turned his gaze back to the papers. "We'll figure it out when we see him. For now, let's go over this together. Make sure we're on the same page before we head in there."

13

Clayton shifted in his seat, feeling the weight of Dawson's glare from across the desk. Being assigned lead on the case meant the responsibility of the report fell squarely on his shoulders, but his unease only grew under the captain's scrutiny. Next to him, Johnson sat stiffly, arms folded, his usual confidence noticeably muted.

"You're saying this girl was killed by her husband?" Dawson leaned forward, resting his elbows on the desk. For a moment, his gaze flicked toward the box of Craig's cookies perched to his right. Clayton caught the glance but said nothing, despite feeling a pang of hunger at the sight.

Clayton opened his mouth to answer, but Johnson cut in. "We're not saying that—yet. We just think it's worth digging deeper into his life."

Dawson sat back, rubbing his chin thoughtfully. "You two need to track down the parent company for this service, Anonyme. We can't have the precinct's reputation tarnished because of this... whatever it is." His tone was sharp as he pointed a thick finger at them both. "Brooks wants this handled, and he wants it kept quiet. Got it?"

Clayton's head jerked up at the mention of the mayor's name, his pulse quickening. "Really? Since when does the mayor get involved in cases here at the precinct?"

Dawson chuckled, though there was little humour in it. "Ever since he's been the one signing off on funding for this place."

"Sam Greene? He's been up to a whole lot." Clayton slid the pages bearing Greene's phone records and the manifests from all the flights he'd taken for last six months.

Dawson eyed the papers with scorn. "You expect me to read all that? Just tell me what you've got, Muttler."

Clayton nodded. "The guy was back in town two days before Evelyn's body was found at 13 Watt Avenue.

Their boss rose from his chair and pointed toward Clayton. "You two find this guy and bring him in for questioning."

CLAYTON GRIPPED THE STEERING WHEEL TIGHTLY, STARING UP AT THE building in front of them. The quiet hum of the Range Rover's engine filled the air as he exhaled sharply. "We should've gone to Evelyn's place the moment we learned who she was. How could I have been so stupid?"

Johnson turned in his seat, his expression skeptical, though his voice remained calm. "Didn't you say Sam Greene's cell phone pinged somewhere else? Not here?" He motioned toward the building with a tilt of his head.

Clayton nodded, rubbing his temple. "Yeah, it did. But that doesn't mean he isn't here now."

Johnson shrugged, unbuckling his seatbelt. "Well, let's hope he is," he said, his tone carrying a mix of sarcasm and optimism.

Clayton glanced at his partner and gave a faint, humourless smile before reaching for the door handle. "Let's find out."

As they approached the entrance to the high-rise, Clayton glanced at his partner. "What do you make of the pathologist's report? If they confirm semen, could it have come from someone at her Anonyme appointment?"

Johnson shoved his hands into his pockets, his brows furrowed in thought. “Maybe. But wouldn’t you think someone like her—a married woman—would’ve taken precautions?”

Clayton grimaced. “Or it could’ve come from her killer, which means she was raped.”

Johnson stopped short at the entrance, placing a firm hand on Clayton’s shoulder. “Hold on. What if Evelyn never made it to her appointment at all?”

14

Clayton and Johnson exchanged glances as Sam Greene collapsed onto the pristine white leather sofa. Evelyn Greene's husband was striking—tall, about six feet, with meticulously groomed hair and manicured nails that spoke of self-discipline and care. His crisp, five-hundred-dollar shirt and the elegant watch he wore hinted at a man who appreciated the finer things in life.

Everything in the apartment was in perfect order, from the minimalist decor to the gleaming surfaces. It felt more like a high-end showroom than a home. Clayton's eyes scanned the space, noting the absence of clutter or any signs of daily life. Even if Sam had extended an invitation for them to sit, Clayton knew he wouldn't take it. The perfection of the setting felt as unwelcoming as the man now seated before them.

Johnson broke the silence first. "Nice place you've got here, Mr. Greene."

Sam exhaled heavily, rubbing his temples. "Thanks," he muttered, his voice barely audible.

Clayton stepped forward, not letting his unease show. "We'd like to ask you a few questions about your wife, Evelyn." His words were measured, but his sharp eyes didn't miss the flicker of emotion that crossed Sam's face at the mention of his dead wife's name.

"We've already talked about this," Sam replied tersely, avoiding their gaze. "I thought Evelyn left me. When I got home yesterday and saw her ring on the bedside table, I felt she decided it was over."

"Isn't that what you've been hoping for?" Johnson said, his tone firm. "We know you didn't return from your trip yesterday. You've been back even before your wife was found dead."

Sam's jaw tightened, and for a brief moment, the tension in the room felt suffocating. Clayton remained steady, silently assessing the man in front of him. Clayton knew what Sam Greene was hiding.

"Fine," Sam muttered, his voice barely above a whisper. "I came back earlier than I said. I had—"

"You were too busy having an affair," Johnson snapped. "Or maybe you were too busy killing your wife!"

Sam's head snapped up, his eyes blazing. "I didn't kill her!" he repeated, louder this time. "Yes, I was having an affair. Yes, our marriage was falling apart. But I'd never hurt her. Never."

Johnson's opened his notepad and leafed through it casually. "Yeah, tell us more about Elian Cruz."

Clayton saw the shock in Sam's eyes. No, it was fear.

"What about him? Elian and I are best friends," Sam replied.

Johnson's smirk widened as he leaned back in his chair, his notepad still open in his hand. "Best friends, huh? That why you've got photos of the two of you in compromising positions on your phone?"

Sam's face drained of colour, his fingers clenching tightly around the armrest of the pristine white sofa. He stammered, "I don't know what you're talking about."

"Cut the act," Clayton interjected, his voice calm but firm. "We've already subpoenaed the phone records. Elian Cruz isn't just your 'best friend,' is he?"

Sam's shoulders sagged. He looked away, avoiding their gaze. "Okay, fine," he muttered, his voice barely above a whisper. "Elian and I... we've been seeing each other for a while."

Johnson moved closer to Sam. "Did Evelyn know about this? Or did she find out and confront you?"

Sam's head snapped up. "Evelyn didn't know. She had no idea about Elian."

Clayton exchanged a glance with Johnson, his expression unreadable. "And Elian? Was he aware of Evelyn?"

"He knew I was married, but he didn't care. It's not like Evelyn and I were happy."

Johnson tapped his pen against his notepad, his tone sharp. "Unhappy or not, she's dead now, Sam. And your little secret affair doesn't exactly paint you in the best light."

Sam's voice cracked as he raised it. "I didn't kill her! I swear, I didn't. Elian had nothing to do with this either."

Clayton's eyes narrowed. "Then you'd better start helping us figure out who did because right now, you're looking guilty as hell."

15

The two detectives had left Sam Greene and headed directly to Elian Cruz's office. Cruz, a young attorney working at a law firm in the heart of the financial district, sat confidently in the glass-enclosed room. As Clayton sat beside Johnson, he could feel they were both thinking the same thing.

Now back in the car, driving to the precinct, Clayton glanced at his partner in the passenger seat. "Was it just me, or did those two guys seem to have a lot in common?"

Johnson grunted, still seeming deep in thought. "They've both got a taste for the finer things," he said.

Clayton nodded. "At least their stories check out. Looks like Sam and Elian have been spending all their time together since his return. And that office screamed money, just like Greene's place." He shook his head, gripping the steering wheel tightly. "Elian Cruz didn't seem fazed by anything we threw at him, though. Cool as a cucumber."

Johnson leaned back in his seat, his expression contemplative. "That's what gets me. The guy's an attorney—he knows how to play it smart. But did you notice the way he dodged certain questions about Sam?"

"He was just protective, I think," Clayton replied. "We both know Sam only married Evelyn to stop his parents from nagging him about getting married and starting a family, being as he's the only son."

Johnson sighed, leaning back in his seat. "So, they were both cool with letting this girl cover for them without her even knowing it."

"But what does that tell us?" Clayton asked as he pulled into the precinct parking lot.

"These guys were together before Greene and Evelyn married," Johnson said thoughtfully. "I can't see either of them wanting her dead. Can you? I mean, Greene even handed over his phone without hesitation for us to go through it."

Clayton shook his head slowly. "Not unless there's something we're missing."

16

Clayton lagged behind Johnson as they entered Civic Tower. It was time to meet the mayor for the first time in his life. Yet, as they approached the elevator, Clayton felt a knot tighten in his chest—he wasn't just meeting the mayor; he was about to meet his father.

Johnson nudged him playfully as they stepped into the elevator. "What's the matter, buddy? Cat got your tongue? You've been quiet ever since we left the car."

"It's all good," Clayton replied, though his voice lacked conviction. His eyes remained fixed on the glowing red numbers above the door, each floor counting down like a timer. With every passing second, the urge to press the emergency button grew stronger.

The elevator doors slid open on the nineteenth floor, revealing a poised assistant waiting for them. For a moment, Clayton and the woman locked eyes, both caught in a silent exchange that made time seem to pause. Johnson, standing at Clayton's side, glanced between the two, raising an eyebrow as he waited for his partner to find his voice.

Clayton, however, found himself uncharacteristically at a loss. The woman standing before them was stunning. Her short, curly hair framed cheekbones reminiscent of Grace Jones—sharp, defined, and striking. Her skin, a deep, smooth ebony, seemed to glow against the crisp white of her tailored pantsuit. The contrast was mesmerizing. But it was her eyes, light brown and piercing, that held him captive. They were unmistakably natural, complementing her warm smile and glossy lips.

Her voice broke the spell, soft yet commanding. "You must be Detective Muttler." She extended a hand, her tone professional but friendly. "I'm Naomi Ellis. Mayor Brooks is expecting you."

Clayton blinked, finally managing to shake her hand. "Yes, that's me. Thank you."

Johnson cleared his throat, stepping forward with a grin. "Rodney Johnson, Clayton's partner," he said, eager to remind everyone he was there.

Naomi's smile widened as she extended her hand toward Johnson. "Nice to meet you, Detective Johnson. We've been expecting you."

Johnson smirked, glancing briefly at the polished floor. "Expecting us? Sure, but only right up to the moment we walked into the building."

Naomi began leading them down the sleek corridor. She glanced back over her shoulder, her smile still bright and genuine. "No, Detective. We've been expecting you since the moment you pulled into the parking lot."

Johnson raised an eyebrow and leaned closer to Clayton, his voice dropping to a whisper. "Oh, she's good," he said with a knowing wink.

Elijah Brooks's office exuded power and prestige, with floor-to-ceiling windows offering an unobstructed view of the city skyline. The sunlight bathed the room in warm light, accentuating the furniture that adorned the expansive space.

Johnson and Clayton entered shoulder to shoulder, following closely behind Naomi. Johnson cast a sidelong glance at his partner, puzzled by the way Clayton had gone uncharacteristically quiet since they stepped into Civic Tower.

The Mayor was nowhere in sight at first, but the deep rumble of his voice filled the room. It came from behind the sleek glass desk near the windows. Elijah Brooks, his tall frame clad in a tailored suit, stood with his back to the door, engrossed in a phone call. His chair sat slightly off-centre, revealing his preference for standing while commanding the room —and, in this case, the city below.

As the detectives approached, the mayor turned slightly, eying them before returning to his conversation. His tone was calm, measured, and authoritative, carrying easily across the office space.

Johnson had never met the mayor before, but Elijah Brooks's reputation was a prominent one. Brooks thrived in the limelight, a natural at commanding attention and respect. For a man in his mid-forties, he radiated a vigour that seemed almost out of place in the world of politics.

His lean, muscular physique was a testament to hours spent in the gym, a habit no doubt cultivated to maintain not only his appearance but his commanding presence. Everything about him exuded youthfulness and energy—a stark contrast to the stereotype of older, weary politicians.

As the mayor finished his phone call and turned toward them, Johnson couldn't help but wonder if the man's charisma was just as powerful in person as it was on the campaign trail.

Brooks acknowledged them only after ending his call, but his attention went straight to Naomi. "Thanks, dear, you're amazing as usual."

Naomi's smile beamed at her boss. "You're expecting these gentlemen to—"

Brooks waved her off with a grin. "Of course!"

He moved directly toward Clayton, extending a hand with practiced confidence. Johnson noticed immediately that Dawson had already prepped the mayor on his rising star.

"Clay Muttler, right?" Brooks said warmly. He shot a brief glance at

Johnson before focusing back on Clayton. "Wade Dawson's said some nice things about you."

Clayton stiffened, seeming unsure how to respond, but managed a polite nod. Johnson could sense the unspoken tension in the room and decided to play it cool, letting Clayton take the lead.

17

Clayton's mother had raised him without a father, working tirelessly to provide everything she thought he needed. But it hadn't been easy—balancing two jobs while raising a child on her own. As Clayton's eyes swept over the mayor's lavish office, the sharp contrast between their lives ignited a sudden surge of anger.

Where had this man, his father, been all his life?

The memories of his life growing up, and his mother's exhausted smile clashed with the opulence surrounding him now.

And yet, as the man stood before him, exuding charm and confidence, it dawned on Clayton with a startling clarity: Elijah Brooks had no idea who he was. His mother had christened him Clayton Hilarion Muttler, choosing the surname from her own mother's maiden name. It was a name steeped in familial pride, a quiet declaration of independence. She had wanted no ties to the man who had fathered him, yet in a twist of irony, her final request before her death had been for Clayton to reveal his identity to this man—a man who remained oblivious to his existence.

Suddenly, the brief moment of silence stretched into what felt like an eternity. Clayton glanced at Naomi, then back to the mayor, before letting his gaze fall on Johnson. Taking a steadying breath, he spoke. "Mr. Mayor," he said, keeping his tone polite but firm, "we'd like to get more information about Evelyn Greene."

The mayor shook his head, a somber expression crossing his face. "Such a shame that this would happen to such a nice girl."

"It's a shame it could happen to anyone at all," Clayton replied, the edge in his voice unintentional but undeniable.

Elijah Brooks's sharp eyes jabbed onto Clayton, and for a moment, the tension in the room seemed to swallow them up. Then, with a soft chuckle, the mayor exhaled. "Of course, detective. All life is precious."

Elijah Brooks turned his back and strode toward his desk. "Naomi will get you everything you need," he said, his tone dismissive. It was a clear signal for them to leave, but Clayton's feet refused to move. Not yet.

"Mr. Brooks," Clayton said, his voice cutting through the heavy silence. He could hear Johnson's sharp intake of breath beside him, a silent warning, but the storm of emotion in Clayton's chest was too much to ignore. Elijah Brooks was his father—a fact Clayton hated, and one he had every reason to.

The mayor turned abruptly, his brow furrowing as his sharp gaze fixed on Clayton. The weight of that look threatened to unbalance him, but Clayton steadied himself and spoke the first words that came to mind. "Thank you for meeting with us, sir."

He was here for Evelyn Greene, not himself. Whatever personal turmoil raged within him could wait.

18

Naomi Ellis led the two detectives to Evelyn Greene's old desk, her steps light, but deliberate. The office was quiet, save for the distant hum of activity, and the space seemed frozen in time, as though Evelyn might return at any moment.

Clayton and Johnson exchanged a glance, a silent conversation passing between them. The younger detective could see the curiosity brewing in his partner's eyes—questions about his tense exchange with the mayor. Clayton knew they were coming, and he braced himself for them once they left Civic Tower.

For now, their focus was Evelyn Greene, and whatever secrets her workspace might reveal.

Johnson motioned toward Evelyn's computer after rummaging through the desk drawers and leafing through several notepads. "Any way we can get into this? We need to check her browsing history."

Clayton understood exactly what his partner was looking for. Evelyn's personal computer at home had revealed no visits to Anonyme's website, and the tech team was still working on extracting data from her cell phone. This computer might hold the missing pieces they needed.

Naomi stepped forward without hesitation and entered the password, the screen flickering to life. “There you go,” she said with a polite smile, stepping aside to let Johnson take over.

Johnson nodded in appreciation and slid into the chair, his fingers moving deftly across the keyboard. “Let’s see what secrets you’ve been hiding, Evelyn,” he muttered under his breath as he began his search.

Clayton moved across the room, scanning Evelyn’s workspace. There was nothing personal—no framed photo of her with Sam Greene, no hint of her family life. It was as if she had carefully curated an image of detachment, a blank slate.

From the corner of his eye, Clayton noticed Naomi moving closer. His stomach tightened. He focused on the shelf in front of him, willing himself not to glance at her. What would he even say if he had to meet those striking brown eyes again?

“So, did you know Evelyn well?” he asked, his voice steady but deliberately casual. He needed something to break the tension building in his chest.

Naomi hesitated, then nodded thoughtfully. “I wouldn’t say we were close, but she was… kind. Evelyn kept things professional. She kept to herself most of the time.” Her tone softened as if she were sharing a secret. “But, you know, I got the feeling there was a lot more to her than what she let on.”

Clayton risked a glance at Naomi. Her expression was contemplative, her beauty even more disarming up close. He quickly looked away, trying to focus on the task at hand.

Clayton pushed his way through the revolving door as he exited Civic Tower, already knowing what Johnson was thinking. Neither of them had uttered a word since leaving the mayor’s office. They were halfway to the Range Rover when Johnson finally snapped.

“What the fuck were you thinking, kid?”

Clayton sighed, his frustration rising as his partner geared up to give him the third degree. He stopped, turned to meet Johnson's glare, and raised his brows in silence.

Johnson jabbed a thumb back toward the glass-fronted building. "You know you pissed the guy off, right? What the hell made you go at him like that?"

"Maybe I just don't like the guy," Clayton muttered as he slid into the driver's seat and slammed the door shut. He stayed quiet, gripping the steering wheel, until Johnson climbed into the passenger seat.

"Dude, you talked to him like he's a suspect in the girl's murder," Johnson said, jabbing a finger toward Civic Tower. "The guy's our fucking boss!"

"Climb off my back, Johnson!" Clayton snapped.

Johnson leaned closer, his voice dropping to a hiss. "So, you go hard at Brooks for no damn reason, but the second a pretty girl shows up, you're all soft."

Clayton felt his face flush hot. His jaw tightened as he turned the key in the ignition, starting the car without saying another word.

19

Elijah Brooks ended his call with Wade Dawson and crossed to the window, where the view overlooked the parking lot below. His eyes locked on the departing Range Rover, its taillights glowing as it disappeared from sight.

He'd called Dawson for two reasons: to gather more details about Evelyn's death and to dig into this new detective.

Something about Clayton Muttler had gotten under his skin, and it wasn't just the man's tone. There was a nagging familiarity about Muttler that Elijah couldn't quite place, and it infuriated him.

Dawson had provided details about Evelyn's actions leading up to her death, and as Elijah mulled over what he'd learned, his gaze lingered on the Range Rover disappearing into the distance.

Dawson had called the young detective clever—ambitious, even—eager to climb the ranks quickly. But to Elijah, the kid seemed to be flying too fast and too high, a dangerous combination in their line of work.

Clayton Muttler was green and eager to make a name for himself—Elijah knew the type well. As a young Black man breaking into politics, Elijah had learned early on that he had to work twice as hard to earn half the respect. He shrugged, a slight smile tugging at the corner of his mouth.

Maybe what he saw in Muttler was a shadow of his younger self. Still, the kid's abrasive attitude was hard to overlook.

Elijah's rise had been swift. At just forty-six, he was running the city, with the entire police force eating out of the palm of his hand. Hard work had paved the way, but he wasn't naïve about the role his wife, Marie, had played in his success. Marrying the daughter of the previous mayor—Civic Tower's so-called king—had been more than a personal milestone; it had been a strategic move.

His thoughts drifted to his family. Three beautiful kids—teenage twin sons and a younger daughter—completed his picture-perfect life. What more could a man ask for?

NAOMI WALKED INTO HIS OFFICE WITHOUT KNOCKING—THE ONLY MEMBER OF his team who dared take such liberty. But Elijah trusted her. She owed him loyalty—the least she could do after he'd opened doors for her that would have otherwise remained shut. Elijah and her father had been close friends for years.

He swivelled in his chair to face her. "What've you got for me, Naomi?"

Naomi tapped her pencil against a notepad, her usual fidgeting betraying her calm exterior. "They asked the usual questions. Evelyn's workspace was exactly as she left it, and I doubt there was anything for them to find."

Elijah noticed the slight pause, the subtle intake of breath, before she moved on to the next topic. "I spoke with our 'contact' at the precinct." She avoided his gaze as she spoke, seeming uncomfortable with the task he'd given her. "Detective Muttler has a clean record. He spent a couple of years as a patrol cop before his recent promotion. Just turned thirty, and his aunt, Ruby Fletcher, is his only emergency contact. He's single."

Her brown eyes flicked up from the notepad, a brief glimmer of hope shining through.

Elijah nodded slowly. Muttler might have seemed like just another regular guy, but something about him still unsettled the mayor. He tugged thoughtfully at his goatee. “Any big leads on Evelyn’s death? What’d our contact have to say about that?”

Naomi hesitated, her eyes flickering briefly as she gathered her thoughts. “Her best friend mentioned a dating service Evelyn might have used... Anonyme, or something like that.”

Elijah’s grip tightened on the arm of his chair. His gaze darkened as he processed the information.

20

Clayton sat at his desk, his eyes locked on the papers spread out before him. He refused to meet Johnson's scrutinizing gaze yet again. With their desks facing each other, there was nowhere else to look but down.

His thoughts drifted, unbidden, to his first meeting with the man who'd fathered him. The memory clawed its way to the surface, reigniting the same fury that had burned in him then.

Elijah Brooks was a charismatic man, but Clayton's gut told him the man was hiding something—maybe even that he was a horrible person. Part of him wanted that to be true.

Standing before his father for the first time had been gut-wrenching. Clayton had searched the man's face, desperate to find some shred of connection—something they shared. But there had been nothing. No shared physical traits, no spark of recognition. All he saw was the deep brown of their skin, a reminder of their distant tie and little else.

Clayton rubbed his temples and closed his eyes, willing the thoughts of his father to dissipate. He exhaled sharply, then turned his attention back to the report in front of him. So far, they had nothing—no leads, no clues, nothing to point them toward Evelyn Greene's killer.

There was a trace of hesitation in Johnson's voice when he spoke. "Look, Muttler, about earlier—if I came off a bit harsh, I—"

Clayton met his gaze, cutting him off. "Don't worry about it."

Johnson studied him for a moment before continuing. "I don't know Brooks all that well, but he's not the kind of boss you mess around with, kid." His eyes brightened slightly, and a faint grin tugged at his lips. "You know, when Dawson first brought you in, I thought you were a little shit. But you're alright. I just don't want you making the wrong moves. Brooks will mess up your career in ways you can't undo if you rub him the wrong way. Take my word for it."

Clayton gave a small nod. "I'll keep that in mind."

But deep down, an unease stirred. Part of him wanted to tell Johnson about his connection to the mayor, to lay it all out and see what his partner thought. Yet, he couldn't bring himself to trust anyone with that truth—not yet.

When Johnson's desk phone rang, it sent a jolt through his chest. His heart thudded against his ribcage as he glanced up.

"Johnson," his partner barked into the receiver, his gaze fixed on Clayton with a sharp intensity. There was a pause, followed by a wide grin spreading across Johnson's face.

He hung up with a snap and sprang to his feet. "Let's move, kid. Nigel from the tech lab's got something new on the CCTV!"

Clayton barely had time to shove the scattered papers aside before Johnson was already heading down the hall. He hurried to keep up, his pulse quickening—not just from the urgency in Johnson's stride, but from the hope that maybe, just maybe, they'd finally caught a break.

THE SURVEILLANCE ANALYST WAS A CHEERFUL YOUNG WOMAN IN HER LATE twenties, but her outward cheerfulness didn't match Clayton's internal discomfort. He sat next to Johnson, across from Tessa Collins's desk, trying to keep his face neutral. He hoped his expression hadn't given him away. Glancing sidelong at Johnson, Clayton felt a pang of annoyance. His partner should have warned him about this meeting—the girl who deliberately crossed out the last letter of her first name. Tess, not Tessa.

Rebelling against the name her parents must've carefully chosen wasn't the strangest thing about her, though.

Tess wore black lipstick and heavy eyeliner, her short-cropped nails polished the same deep shade. The girl was clearly goth, and while Clayton could appreciate the boldness, he found it impossible to focus on anything else. Every detail seemed designed to pull his attention. Her tongue flicked nervously as she absentmindedly played with her tongue ring, a small, intrusive motion Clayton couldn't shake from his mind.

Her arm tattoos were vibrant, and the ink snaking up her neck was just as loud, just as impossible to ignore. But it was her ears that made Clayton cringe. They were pierced along the entire length of each, a detail that felt overwhelming and inescapable every time he looked at her.

He forced his gaze back to her face, trying to remind himself why they were here: the information she had was vital.

Tess smiled at Johnson, and Clayton could tell they were well acquainted. "You were right about this one, Rodney," she said, her eyes flicking to Clayton as she passed him a manila folder.

Johnson grinned and nudged Clayton playfully. "Told her you'd be a little put off by her style."

Clayton smiled shyly, meeting Tess's piercing blue gaze. "Well, yeah... I was a bit surprised, you know?"

Tess didn't seem offended at all. If anything, she seemed amused. "I grew up being daddy's little girl—until I started expressing myself." She raised her arms slightly, gesturing to her black attire and tattoos. "My dad was a pastor, and when he saw this, he thought I was the incarnation of Satan himself. Suddenly, I wasn't his little girl anymore. So, when I turned eighteen, I decided I'd rather be me. I see my mom once a year, but I haven't spoken to Reverend Collins since I moved out."

Clayton sat silently, the weight of her words sinking in. His thoughts drifted involuntarily to his own estranged father.

Once again, it was Johnson who cut the tension. "So, Tess... what've you got for us?"

TESS FLIPPED HER MONITOR TOWARD THE TWO DETECTIVES, A GRIN PLAYING at her lips. "You guys won't believe what I've got on our vic, Evelyn Greene. It's basically the last few hours of her life." She struck a few keys on her keyboard, and the blurry video popped up on the screen. "I set it up to play in sequence, from the moment she left her building."

Clayton stared, his mouth slightly agape. He could hear Johnson whistle under his breath, but neither of them spoke as they watched.

Evelyn Greene appeared on the screen, dressed in a simple but striking outfit—a dark dress, maybe black or deep navy. The fabric looked thin, almost like lingerie, with delicate spaghetti straps that reminded Clayton of Anonyme's billboard advertisement. In that moment, he realized something with a jolt: the billboard was powerful enough to make Evelyn want to emulate the woman in it.

The black box she held was large enough to require both hands, but Clayton suspected it was light. Evelyn moved with graceful ease, the kind of quiet confidence that made her seem untouchable. She headed north on Alder Street, only stopping four blocks away at Cypress Avenue.

She didn't wait long. A black Tesla arrived within a minute, its left gullwing door swinging open. Evelyn placed the box in first, then slid into the back seat. The car continued northward, disappearing out of view.

Clayton leaned forward in his chair, watching the Tesla drive off. He noticed Johnson doing the same.

"Well, we got ourselves a plate number," Johnson said, turning to Clayton, his voice bright with excitement. "Our first big lead, kid!"

PART II

21

He had taken every precaution to ensure nothing could be traced back to him. Perfection demanded discipline—timing, precision, and above all, privacy. Rushing was for amateurs, and amateurs got caught.

The room was massive and sterile, its white walls gleaming under the harsh, clinical lights. He needed light—lots of it. Within this sanctuary, it was impossible to tell if it was day or night, but he kept meticulous track of time. Timing was everything.

Standing at the centre of the room, he took a deep breath, surveying the culmination of his efforts. Everything was perfect.

But there were no mirrors. No reflective surfaces. He made sure of that. He never wanted to see his own face.

His gaze shifted to her. For a moment, he admired the stillness, the way her features softened in unconsciousness. She looked so peaceful. But it wouldn't last. The sedative would wear off soon, and she would awaken. Then, her final moments would begin.

He allowed himself a brief smile. *I will be the last thing she sees. The last voice she hears. The last pair of eyes she meets.*

The tools of his craft were laid out in precise order on the steel table.

Not a single instrument was out of place. There was no room for chaos here—this was his sacred place.

He moved toward her with deliberate, silent steps, his heart quickening as he approached. As he looked down at her, unconscious and vulnerable, his adrenaline surged.

To him, she was a blank canvas, waiting for his artistry to begin. He would make her beautiful. More perfect than the last one.

She would be his second masterpiece. The ones before them—they didn't count. They were practice, trials that had taught him precision and restraint. He had discarded them easily, yet he had not forgotten where they rested. Their presence lingered in his mind, markers of his evolution.

His gaze lingered on the girl, barely twenty-five. Her name didn't matter; it never did. Names added weight, and he had no room for that.

A flicker of movement—the slightest flutter of her eyelids—sent a thrill coursing through him. Soon, she would wake. Anticipation tightened in his chest. He leaned close, inhaling deeply, catching her unique scent. He let it fill him, closing his eyes to savour the moment. This, the moment before, was always exquisite.

Stepping back, he allowed himself to truly look at her. The gentle rise and fall of her chest, her slender waist, the way her full breasts seemed to defy gravity. She was a canvas of perfection, raw and unspoiled.

The thought flickered briefly—a temptation, a primal urge to take her as she was. To ruin the purity of the moment. But no. He clenched his fists, forcing the impulse down.

Patience.

It was always better when he waited. Always better when they saw him.

HER HEAD THROBBED, AND AS HER EYES FLUTTERED OPEN, SHE SQUINTED against the blinding glare of the pot lights above. The room spun in a blur, her vision struggling to adjust. Then she saw him—a figure moving in the periphery, barely audible but profoundly menacing.

Panic clawed at her chest as she tried to piece together where she was, how she'd gotten here. Her mind jogged through fragmented memories, but nothing made sense. She raised a trembling hand to rub her eyes, but it felt like lifting lead. Her body was too weak, too heavy to resist as the warmth of his palm slid with deliberate slowness up her leg.

Her breaths came shallow and rapid as his shadow loomed over her. His face was close now, too close. *Why is he doing this? Why me?*

The weight of him pressed down, crushing her chest with its unbearable presence. His breath, hot and steady, brushed against her face, each exhale more terrifying than the last. She tried to speak, to scream, but the sound lodged in her throat, strangled by fear.

His hands moved deliberately, creeping up her arms, circling her neck with dreadful precision. Her pulse thundered in her ears, her vision narrowing as he worked.

And then, she felt it—the smooth texture of something sliding around her throat. A cord? A belt? Her mind couldn't process it. The rhythm of his breathing quickened, almost matching the frantic drumbeat of her heart.

Her gaze locked on his, pleading, but his eyes betrayed nothing—no pity, no hesitation, only a cold, mechanical focus.

The pressure tightened, and just as the pieces began to snap together in her mind, the lights seemed to flicker. Then, darkness took her.

HE STRAIGHTENED, HIS MUSCLES ACHING SLIGHTLY FROM THE EFFORT OF immersing the body—his canvas—into the steaming bath. The cleanup process was tedious, a mundane necessity in his otherwise thrilling masterpiece. But it was essential. No mistakes. No evidence. There could be no trace of him left behind. But he was no fool. He knew there were ways to find the the smallest trace of him.

The heat of the water had already begun its work, softening her, purging her of impurities. Her pale skin appeared almost luminous against the murky bathwater, angelic if not for the red, angry marks around her neck. Those, too, would be remedied soon enough.

He lingered for a moment, admiring the way the rising steam shrouded her, a veil of secrecy over his creation. But there was no time to waste, the clock was ticking.

Pulling a pair of latex gloves over his hands, the sharp snap echoed in the sterile room. His gaze shifted to the neatly arranged tools on the counter—makeup, brushes, and powders meticulously placed in anticipation.

It was time to begin the transformation.

22

It was Saturday morning, and Clayton lay in bed, staring at the cracks on the ceiling like they might offer answers. His mind was a labyrinth of haunting thoughts, all leading back to one man: Elijah Brooks, his father. The mayor. The ghost he couldn't escape.

The idea of confronting him, as his mother had wanted, lingered like an itch he couldn't scratch. Should he tell Elijah the truth? Should he look the man in the eye and let him know they were kin? He had always told himself he didn't care, that it didn't matter. But that was a lie, wasn't it?

Some part of him—a small, aching part—wanted to know this man. To see himself reflected in his father's face. Yet another part felt that it wasn't worth it. Elijah Brooks had been just sixteen years old when he was born, practically a kid himself. What did he know about fatherhood back then? What would he care now?

Clayton's jaw tightened, the weight of the morning pressing down on him like the silence of the room. No, Elijah Brooks never wanted him. That much he was sure of.

Clayton rubbed his eyes, cursing softly under his breath as though someone might hear him. But he was alone, lying on his unmade bed in a room lit only by the faint morning light seeping through the blinds. The haze of his restless thoughts lingered—Elijah Brooks, his father, always hovering at the edges of his mind.

The sharp ring of his cell phone broke through the quiet, yanking him out of his spiral. He grabbed it off the nightstand, glancing briefly at the screen before pressing it to his ear.

Dawson's voice hit him like a horsewhip. "You need to drag your ass out of bed and get down to Saint Michael's. Pronto!"

Clayton blinked, confused, his thoughts still sluggish. "It's Saturday," he muttered, his voice gravelly. "My day off. What's so important?"

"Another case," Dawson snapped, his words garbled like he was chewing on something. "And this one's big."

Clayton sat up straighter, suddenly more awake. "Another break in Evelyn Greene's case?"

"No, Muttler. It's another case entirely." Dawson's voice dropped slightly, carrying a weight that made Clayton's stomach twist. "But it has her killer's signature all over it."

Clayton arrived at Saint Michael's Church to find Dawson and Johnson already on site. Yellow police tape stretched across the entrance like a warning, keeping back a growing crowd of onlookers. Among them stood the priest, his expression a tight mix of concern and quiet resignation.

Clayton hadn't thought to stop for coffee, and as he approached, Dawson's eyes flicked to his empty hands, his disappointment almost palpable.

Clayton grimaced. Yeah, showing up with coffee and something sweet might've softened the blow of his tardiness, but what did Dawson expect? That he'd skip a shower and roll in unkempt? Not a chance.

He offered his boss a curt nod, then shot Johnson a sharp look—silent payback for not calling him first.

"Morning," Clayton muttered, tilting his chin toward the church entrance. "What are we looking at?"

Johnson shot Clayton a glance, something flickering behind his eyes—jealousy, maybe. "What we're looking at, kid, is a possible serial killer. A case like this can make a man's career... or break it." His tone was edged with doubt, as if he wasn't sure which way Clayton would fall.

Before Clayton could respond, Dawson's voice sliced through the tension. "The ME's just about finished. Let's move."

Clayton fell in step behind them, bracing himself for another long day. Cases like this had a way of sinking their teeth in, refusing to let go.

THE THREE MEN PASSED FELLOW OFFICERS AS THEY WALKED THROUGH THE double doors and made their way up the nave. Sunlight filtered through the stained glass windows, casting fractured colours across the stone floor, giving the space an almost ethereal glow. The high ceilings of Saint Michael's loomed above them, amplifying the silence—eerie, oppressive, and expectant.

Clayton's thoughts returned to the day of his mother's funeral, his steps faltering. Saint Michael's was his mother's church.

Looking ahead, Clayton saw why Dawson and Johnson had seemed disturbed when he arrived. There was a body on the floor of the transept.

Dawson spoke in a low, solemn tone as they moved closer. "My kids were christened here, for God's sake. Why would this guy do such a thing here of all places?"

Johnson grunted. "Because he's crazy and has no respect, that's why."

She was Caucasian, mid-twenties, and looked almost perfect in death. This was Clayton's first observation. His gut told him, once again, that the killer was meticulous and deliberate. That's the impression the crime scene left on him as soon as he stepped closer to the poor girl.

She was naked, her skin pale—almost translucent. Clayton could tell the killer had chosen her carefully, and he was certain her flawless appearance had been enhanced by the steady hand of a murderer, like an artist with an airbrush.

She looked almost angelic, lying there in the centre of the transept, where the nave and sanctuary intersected, forming a cross.

The three men studied the scene in silence, and Clayton noticed that Dawson and Johnson, despite clearly having seen the scene before, were reacting as if this was the first time.

Clayton couldn't keep his thoughts to himself any longer. Pointing toward the victim's outstretched arms, he shook his head, a sad realization settling in. "It's all symbolic. He's positioned her like a crucifixion—arms outstretched. She's been crucified."

Dawson stared at him, almost in awe of his observation. "But she ain't got no wounds, does she?"

Clayton nodded slowly. "No. But if this is the same guy, I'm willing to bet the strangle marks are buried beneath all that perfect makeup."

Johnson let out his signature whistle. "Damn, look at how natural she looks. It's like he's made her innocent again. But how the hell does he get her in here without anyone noticing?"

Clayton shrugged, frustration evident in his expression. "It's a church, open 24/7, but I'd bet my lunch we won't find a trace of him or her on the CCTV—just like the last one."

23

Dawson walked into the mayor's office at Civic Tower, wondering why Brooks had requested to see him in person. As Brooks's assistant, Naomi Ellis, exited the room, Dawson couldn't help but admire her. Bigwigs always seemed to have access to the most attractive women.

Realizing he had been staring, he turned back to face the mayor, feeling a flicker of embarrassment. He was a married man, but looking never hurt—at least, that's what he told himself.

"Mayor." He lowered himself into the chair across from Brooks's desk without waiting for an invitation.

"I hear you've got yourself another busy day, Wade." Brooks leaned back in his chair.

Dawson shook his head. "Yeah, we're certain it's the same guy. Same MO."

Brooks seemed on edge, and Dawson again wondered why he'd been summoned for a conversation that could have easily happened over the phone.

"Any big leads yet?" Brooks asked.

Dawson scratched his chin, noting how carefully Brooks chose his words. "Muttler and Johnson were at the scene with me this morning," he said with a sigh, debating just how much of the case he should reveal. "Evelyn Greene was a normal girl—had a normal life... and it's safe to say we can rule out the husband and his boyfriend."

Brooks's brows lifted. "Boyfriend?"

Dawson tilted his head slightly. "Look, it's complicated, but I ain't one to judge."

His gaze drifted past Brooks, settling on a large canvas hanging on the wall. Like the rest of the office, the artwork was exquisite—too expensive to have been bought with taxpayer money.

Brooks's voice pulled him back. "And this other victim?"

"It's definitely the same killer," Dawson said. "Muttler thinks this guy will just keep getting more extreme."

Brooks cleared his throat, rubbing his palms together. "You think this new kid—Muttler—is good for the case?"

"The kid's got balls, and he's smart." Dawson studied his boss, trying to figure out where he was going with this.

Brooks sighed. "The press has been calling Civic Tower all day, Wade." He pointed a finger across his desk. "We need details for them, or we'll look like idiots."

"I'll put our PR team on it," Dawson offered.

"No need—I already arranged it." Brooks smirked. "Press conference at five o'clock. Let's see how your golden boy handles it."

Dawson leaned forward. "Elijah, the kid's green."

"You say he's got balls?" Brooks leaned back. "Then throw him to the wolves and see how he does."

Dawson exhaled slowly. "Oh, I see. Johnson told me the kid was a bit of a smart-ass with you yesterday."

Brooks's smirk didn't waver. "Just put him before the press."

Dawson nodded. Brooks was the boss.

24

The two detectives sat across from each other at their desks, rummaging through papers as they compared the similarities between the two murders. Clayton was convinced both women had been killed by the same person.

Like Evelyn Greene, the second victim was a mystery. She had been left inside Saint Michael's Church, positioned with deliberate care—lying on her back, her face turned toward the heavens. Her ankles were crossed, and her arms outstretched, as if she had been nailed to a cross.

Clayton had climbed to the gallery, studying the scene from above. From that vantage point, the symbolism became undeniable. The killer had placed her at the exact centre of the transept. Viewed from above, the positioning gave the illusion of crucifixion—an eerie, calculated statement.

They were still waiting on the medical examiner's report, but Clayton already expected it to mirror Evelyn Greene's.

Across the desk, Johnson looked up from his paperwork, his tone softer than usual. "That plate from the Tesla came back clean. I had Phillips double-check ownership with the DMV."

Clayton nodded, but his thoughts drifted back to the victim—her face, frozen in unnatural peace, lying in the centre of Saint Michael's.

Dawson's voice snapped him back. "Hey, listen up, boys." His gaze locked onto Clayton. "This thing at the church has everyone losing their minds, and something tells me that's exactly what our guy wanted. This son of a bitch likes attention, so let's humour him—give him a little taste."

Johnson rubbed his palms together. "Not like we've got much to give, do we? He's pulling all the strings while we're just trying to catch up." Frustration flared as he slapped his desk.

Dawson pointed directly at Clayton. "You're taking lead on this. Press conference. Five o'clock."

Clayton's heart kicked in his chest. He was a detective—crime scenes, evidence, tracking killers—that was his job. Not TV, not the spotlight. His mind flickered to the mayor's polished media presence, and in that moment, he realized just how little he had in common with his father.

CLAYTON WATCHED PHILLIPS AS HE WALKED AWAY FROM HIS DESK. THE records clerk looked to be around twenty-five, but nothing about his appearance suggested he was just administrative. Phillips was built like a football player, yet his demeanour was that of a gentle giant. He was black, soft-spoken, but efficient.

Johnson was watching him with a sly grin. "Not everything is as it seems, is it, kid?" He laughed, gesturing toward the elevator, where Phillips was waiting.

"He's very thorough," Clayton said, lifting the report Phillips had just delivered. "And a man of few words."

Johnson's look hardened as he leaned in, his voice low. "You think he's our guy? You think he killed those girls?" He suddenly burst into loud laughter, making heads turn in their direction.

Clayton grinned. "You're an idiot, you know that, Johnson?"

Johnson lifted both arms as if accepting cheers from an invisible crowd. "No, seriously, Phillips is a good kid. Came to us right out of college."

Clayton tapped the report against his desk. "So, we've got the owner of the Tesla. When do we do this?"

"Well, kid," Johnson said, leaning back in his chair, "you've got that press conference in a couple of hours... no sense in leaving now. We could pay this guy a visit first thing in the morning."

25

Clayton stood next to Johnson in the elevator, not knowing what to expect. It was his first press conference, and although Dawson had assured him it would be easy, Clayton had his doubts.

"Remember, kid, don't give out anything that could help the killer," Johnson said, keeping his gaze fixed on the red digits above the elevator door as they counted down.

Clayton nodded, though his thoughts were already elsewhere.

"Some of these reporters can be jerks," Johnson warned. "Don't let them piss you off. Remember, we're on TV."

Fear began to build inside Clayton, but he simply took a deep breath and kept quiet, trying to ignore the anxiety curling in his stomach.

The elevator stopped, and the doors opened. Clayton's eyes were immediately drawn to the group of reporters gathered at the bottom of the steps ahead. His heart sank. The sight of them sent a wave of panic through him. But that wasn't all. Standing before a wooden lectern was Elijah Brooks, the mayor himself. To his father's left stood Dawson.

Clayton froze for a moment. His first instinct was to turn back, but he had little time to gather his thoughts.

Before he could process the situation, he felt a gentle touch on his arm.

He turned to see Naomi Ellis. She smiled at him, her presence a calming contrast to the chaos. "You're right there," she said, pointing toward a piece of tape on the floor, just to the right of the lectern, beside his father.

The blinding lights and constant flashes from cameras made Clayton's head spin. He could feel the sweat beading on his forehead, the press of expectation surrounding him. He gave Naomi a nod as she gently guided him into place. Her touch was soothing, a small anchor in the sea of overwhelming sensations.

Johnson, positioned to Clayton's right, seemed at ease. He'd done this before. But for Clayton, every moment felt like a battle against his nerves.

STANDING NEXT TO THE MAYOR, CLAYTON WONDERED WHAT THE REPORTERS would think if they knew the detective to his right was actually his son. He felt the weight of his father's presence—his commanding voice, his polished confidence, the sheer power he exuded. Yet Elijah Brooks remained oblivious to the truth.

Clayton forced those thoughts away, only realizing he had curled his hands into fists when his nails dug into his palms. He unclenched them, exhaling slowly. Now wasn't the time.

The mayor's baritone voice pulled him back to reality. "The safety of our city is paramount. We will not let anyone rob us of the peace we have." Brooks gripped the lectern like a preacher at the pulpit, his conviction unwavering. The sight of it made Clayton's hidden rage simmer.

Every eye in the room was fixed on the mayor—he knew how to command an audience. With a practiced gesture, Brooks motioned to his left, introducing Dawson. Then, as he turned right, Clayton heard his name. Instinct forced him to meet his father's gaze.

"I have full confidence in the work and experience of our lead in this case, Detective Clay Muttler," the mayor announced smoothly. "And we also have Detective Johnson on this."

The way he said it made Clayton feel less like a detective and more like one of the priceless artifacts decorating his father's office—something to display, something to use.

He didn't like it.

Elijah Brooks had monologued for nearly thirty minutes without a thought of allowing Dawson to utter a word. Clayton's eyes shifted briefly to his left. The mayor loved his own voice. It took every ounce of restraint for Clayton to keep from opening the floor to questions himself. It wouldn't have looked good if he had. Besides, it wasn't as if he was eager to answer them.

At last, the mayor's endless speech ceased, but then Clayton heard it—his name, spilling from his father's mouth. There was something about the way he said it, a slow, deliberate weight to it, that made his skin crawl.

"I'm sure you all have questions." Elijah Brooks chuckled at his own comment, as if the thought amused him. "So, why don't we let Detective Muttler take the lead from here?" He turned to Clayton with a nod, firm and expectant.

A rustling of movement swept across the room as hands shot into the air, fingers clenched around pens and poised pencils, eager to scribble down every word. For a moment, Clayton only stared, his pulse a heavy drum in his ears. Then it hit him—he had to pick someone.

He pointed at the tall man at the back, a fellow with albinism. Clayton found his uniqueness striking, but it was the intensity in his green eyes that compelled him to select him first.

"Thank you, detective." The reporter pulled his pencil from his blonde afro, and Clayton couldn't help but smile. The fellow was the only reporter using a Blackwing 602. Clayton knew the pencils well—they were his favourite.

"What kind of suspect profile are investigators working with? And if

Evelyn Greene's killer is still out there, why do authorities believe they struck again now?"

Clayton liked the question, but he knew he had to be careful with his answer. He locked eyes with the reporter as he responded. "Based on statistical trends in violent crimes, this individual is likely male, between the ages of 30 and 50. He is highly intelligent, deliberate, and somewhat ritualistic."

Clayton took a breath, momentarily forgetting the crowded room. He focused solely on the reporter. "This person is calculated, and we believe them to be a serial killer."

The reporter nodded. "So you believe this is someone who has killed before?"

"The killings and the placement of the victims were too precise to be firsts," Clayton replied. "So yes, we believe this person has killed before."

He selected another reporter closer to the front. She kept her gaze on her notepad as she asked, "Have any new witnesses come forward regarding either case?"

Clayton gave nothing away, though his thoughts immediately went to Monica Sinclair. "We'd rather keep that information private at this time." He moved on, nodding toward another reporter.

"What measures are being taken to prevent further violence at Saint Michael's?"

"We've placed uniformed officers at both locations where the victims were found." Another nod.

"What new evidence, if any, has come to light regarding Evelyn Greene's murder?"

Clayton shrugged, keeping his expression neutral. "All information on evidence in both cases is classified at this time." He flashed a playful grin. "But it will be made public in court as soon as our killer is apprehended."

The same reporter, a woman in her thirties, pressed him further. "But do you believe you can catch him?"

Clayton had no doubt. He met her gaze without hesitation. "Yes, I do. I'm certain of it. Careful and methodical as this person is, everyone makes mistakes. Everyone slips up."

26

Elijah Brooks headed toward the exit of the precinct promptly after the press conference, not sparing Dawson a single glance. Several reporters stopped him along the way, but the mayor seemed practiced at keeping his responses brief when it suited him.

As Naomi passed through the door, she glanced back, her eyes meeting Clayton's. It was as though she knew he was watching her. They exchanged a lingering look—something unspoken but clear—before Clayton pressed his lips together and gave a subtle nod. He couldn't forget how gentle her touch had felt on his arm earlier.

The moment was shattered by the gruff sound of Johnson's voice. "That one's hot for you, kid," he said with a grin. "It's written all over her face."

Dawson still stood with them, giving Clayton an approving smile as he pointed at him. "I knew you could do it, Muttler. Good job!" Before walking away, he slapped Clayton's shoulder. "It's always good to prove the doubters wrong, kid."

Johnson whistled, suddenly amused. "Are you serious, Dawson? You mean Brooks wanted him to crash out?"

Dawson shot Johnson a scathing look. "And you should know when to keep your mouth shut. The vultures are still buzzing around."

As Dawson led the way toward the elevator, Clayton heard his name called.

"Detective Muttler." The voice was familiar.

Turning, Clayton saw the reporter he'd selected earlier. He motioned for Dawson and Johnson to go on without him.

The reporter's green eyes were penetrating, glinting with curiosity. He extended a pale hand toward Clayton, and their grips met with firm resolve. "I'm Elliot Frost with *The Sentinel Review*."

Clayton recognized the name of the paper but had little time for anything but case files and reports lately. "Good to meet you, Elliot. I'm Clayton."

Elliot's grin flashed a row of perfect white teeth. "Can I call you Clay?"

Clayton raised an eyebrow but shrugged. "What can I do for you, Elliot?" He found the reporter friendly enough, but he'd had a long day and wanted to get straight to the point.

"We should talk about what we can do for each other," Elliot said, his tone almost playful. "You know, share information from time to time."

Clayton held his response for a moment, studying Elliot. He tilted his head slightly, as if trying to seem indifferent, but something in his gut told him Elliot Frost was a damned good reporter. "I'm listening."

27

Clayton pulled into the parking lot of Westbridge Executive Transport. The high-security garage was nestled in the city's elite district—Warehouse 7, Kingsley Docks.

He knew exactly how the first part of his day would go. They had tracked down the owner of the Tesla that picked up Evelyn Greene at Alder Street and Cypress Avenue.

As expected, Johnson was already there, sitting in his car, staring at the massive warehouse. Clayton pulled in beside him and got out, taking in the two-story structure by the water. Its design was sleek, exclusive—glass walls revealing glimpses of luxury vehicles lined up like museum pieces.

Johnson let out a low whistle, his thoughts mirroring Clayton's. "This place is a damn menagerie of expensive rides." He climbed out of his car, joining Clayton at the front of his Range Rover.

"Yeah," Clayton murmured. "But inside that building is the car that picked up Evelyn Greene the day she died."

"Or the day before," Johnson countered. He nodded toward the massive sign looming over the aircraft-hangar-style doors.

"Let's see what Westbridge Executive Transport has to say about their cars, their clients... and murder."

ANONYME

Mitchell Milan, founder and owner of Westbridge Executive Transport, looked to be around the same age as the mayor—mid-forties. He was tall but stood several inches shorter than Clayton, his physique lean and youthful despite his age. Though his features retained a certain vitality, his prematurely white hair suggested a man who had seen more than he let on.

The man carried himself with the air of an authoritative teacher—the kind that made you instinctively want to add *Mister* before his name. His calm, stern eyes studied the detectives, making Clayton feel as though he needed permission to speak before stating their purpose.

Clayton sat to Johnson's right, across from Mr. Milan's desk, inside an office surrounded by glass. From here, the owner had the perfect vantage point of the massive garage below.

Earlier, as they were led inside, Clayton had counted at least fifteen luxury cars—each one worth more than he'd make in a few years.

Mr. Milan leaned back slightly, his gaze steady. "What can I do for you, gentlemen?"

Johnson took the lead, and Clayton was glad for it. He wanted to observe Milan carefully.

"I'm pretty sure you know why we're here, Mr. Milan," Johnson said, his gaze locked on the man's stern brown eyes. "We've got intel that puts two dead girls inside your cars." He gestured toward the showroom below.

Clayton resisted the urge to glance at his partner, careful not to betray the half-truth. Johnson was fishing—trying to pry loose anything about the second murder. Neither of them had actual evidence linking the cases, but if the second victim had also been a client at Anonyme, then they'd be onto something big.

Before Milan could respond, Johnson slid a neatly folded sheet of paper across the glass desk.

"That there, Mr. Milan, is a search warrant. Signed by a judge. All we need are the booking details—and a look at that pretty black Tesla."

Milan didn't glance at the warrant. His eyes stayed locked on Johnson.

"We run a car service, Detective... what's your name again?"

"Johnson."

Milan nodded, his grin both mischievous and cooperative. "Right. We get a booking, we send the cars. It's that simple."

Clayton leaned forward. "So, do all your clients request driverless cars?"

Milan's gaze snapped to him, his glare sharper than expected. Then, just as quickly, a smooth smile erased the flicker of irritation.

"Only two clients require self-driving cars," he said, arching a brow. "They can afford it."

Clayton nodded. "How often does your company fulfill requests for Anonyme?"

He saw it—the flash of recognition in Milan's eyes.

Milan adjusted a miniature samurai sculpture on his desk, as if it had somehow shifted out of place. "Look, they're our biggest client. And yeah, I know what they do... hell, I've even used their service." No hesitation. No discomfort. "The service is completely discreet. We never get details on who the cars pick up."

Johnson cut in, still fishing. "Two women were killed after using this service, and your cars picked them up. How does this self-driving thing work, anyhow? These things reliable?"

What happened next surprised Clayton. Milan perked up. His tongue loosened, his voice gaining energy. Was it pride? Ego?

He leaned forward, eyes bright. "These cars all have autonomous capabilities, but our biggest client needed more. So, I took things a step further—introduced a custom Self-Driving System. The best AI aftermarket system ever built."

Milan settled back in his chair, steepling his fingers beneath his chin.

"No need for hands on the wheel. My cars just take you places."

28

Back at the precinct, Clayton found himself once again seated across from Tessa Collins's desk. He thought he'd grown accustomed to the way she flicked her tongue ring against her teeth, but today, it grated on him. Maybe it was the fatigue. Maybe it was knowing they were running out of time.

Tess had struck out on CCTV footage near Saint Michael's, but she'd uncovered something far more valuable: a name for their latest Jane Doe.

While Clayton and Johnson had been questioning Mitchell Milan, someone had come forward to report a missing person. Sabine Aldrich had last been seen two days before her body was found at the church. Clayton had a photo of her in hand—the one her boyfriend had provided. He'd chosen it over the coroner's shots. He didn't need to see Sabine in death again. He needed to remember her as she was in life.

Tess's fingers moved swiftly over her keyboard, her screen flickering with the footage she was pulling up. Clayton kept his focus on the photo. Sabine had been beautiful. Blonde, mid-twenties, a slight tilt to her head as if caught mid-laugh. Now she was another victim in a case that was getting darker by the hour.

"From what Milan told us, you should see a black Lamborghini Urus," he said, finally breaking the silence.

Tess arched a brow and let out a low whistle. "Sounds like an expensive way to die." She bit at a chipped nail, eyes scanning the footage. "Just think—go to some posh place to get laid, and next thing you know, you're dead."

Johnson shook his head. "Nah. We don't even know if Evelyn and Sabine made it to that place—wherever the hell it is."

Clayton stroked his goatee, eyes narrowing. "But we'll know soon, won't we?"

Johnson pointed at him. "I'm telling you, kid, we should've pressed Milan for the GPS data on that Tesla while we had him. I had the guy eating out of my hand."

"I agree," Clayton admitted. "But a warrant guarantees he doesn't wipe anything clean. Let him think we're done with him."

Johnson grinned, rubbing his hands together. "Then we hit him where it hurts."

Clayton just nodded, his mind already moving ahead. Milan had been confident—too confident. But everyone made mistakes. And their killer? He was bound to slip up.

"BINGO!" TESS SNAPPED HER FINGERS AND FLIPPED HER MONITOR TOWARD them. "Your car guy was telling the truth, then," she said with a grin.

Clayton leaned forward, eager to see the last footage of Sabine Aldrich alive. "Rosemont and Vale," he muttered, noting how similar the footage looked to Evelyn's. Sabine held the black box with both hands, struggling to balance it as she opened the rear door of the luxurious car. The lights of the Lamborghini Urus glowed brightly as a veil of darkness slowly fell over the streets. "She was picked up later than Evelyn."

Tess nodded. "Yep. Time stamp shows 9:48 PM. And that area is super high-end, with a nightlife made for the wealthy."

Johnson clicked his tongue, tapping the monitor with his thick forefinger. "This girl was rich," he said, turning to Clayton. "Did you see the threads her boyfriend was wearing?" He shook his head, looking perplexed. "The guy was pretty good-looking. Why would Sabine wanna use Anonyme? They're both young."

"Get with the program, Rodney." Tess waved a finger at him. "Maybe they had an arrangement. You know... 'you can play, but keep it to yourself' kinda thing."

Clayton shook his head, not liking where the dialogue was going. "She had money, but how does Anonyme decide what car to send?"

"Kid, you're right!" Johnson dragged a hand through his disheveled hair. "That Lamborghini's gotta be well over two hundred grand."

Clayton kept watching, seeing Sabine enter the car and pull the door shut before it rolled south on Rosemont. "Let's hope we get that warrant soon," he said. "We need to find out where those cars went, and fast."

Tess grinned at Johnson as she spoke. "So, what'd Super Bowl find out?"

Clayton looked between them, puzzled, feeling left out of their inside joke.

Johnson chuckled, tapping Clayton's shoulder. "Tess gives certain people nicknames," he admitted. "She's asking about Phillips... you know, small voice, football player build."

The two laughed simultaneously, leaving Clayton shaking his head with a grin. But his thoughts quickly returned to what the records clerk had learned about Anonyme's parent company.

"Mitchell Milan told us Anonyme is under the Orbis Noir umbrella."

"And we're talking tons of money," Johnson added. "Business records show the whole shebang is owned and operated by Livia Castellan."

Tess shrugged nonchalantly. "Am I supposed to know who that is?"

Clayton chuckled at her expression, liking Tess more by the minute. "We've never heard of her either." He glanced at the clock on the wall. "Which means we'd better get moving and pay Livia Castellan a visit first thing tomorrow morning."

Clayton sat in the passenger seat of Johnson's sedan, feeling trapped. Johnson's foot hit the accelerator, and the car lurched forward again. Clayton regretted not taking his Range Rover. His knees pressed uncomfortably against the dashboard, but he forced himself to focus on the task at hand. They were on their way to pay Livia Castellan a surprise visit.

Johnson changed lanes abruptly, barely checking his mirrors. "What the hell is Orbis Noir?" His thick fingers drummed against the steering wheel.

Clayton had committed everything he'd learned about Livia Castellan to memory. "It's Latin and French—means '*Black World.*'"

Johnson smirked. "Sounds like a fitting name for Anonyme's parent company, doesn't it?"

Clayton nodded, gripping the door as Johnson weaved through traffic. "Sophisticated and secret. It also fits its owner's name."

Finally, Johnson swung into the parking lot of 299 Dominion Street. Clayton peered out at the towering glass building, its sleek facade reflecting the busy city streets below. Pedestrians and business executives moved with purpose, weaving between high-end boutiques and exclusive storefronts. He looked up at the words Orbis Noir emblazoned near the top of the tower.

"I've passed this place a hundred times," he murmured, "but I've never really noticed it until now."

29

A male secretary led the two detectives down a long, pristine hallway toward Livia Castellan's office. As they walked, Clayton glanced at Johnson, wondering if he'd noticed the same things he had. They followed the man in silence, but the slight lift of Johnson's brows confirmed it—he'd noticed too.

From the moment they passed security, Clayton had picked up on the unusual gender imbalance. Of the ten employees they'd passed so far, only two were women. He hadn't met Livia Castellan yet, but he could hardly wait.

The secretary escorted them through opaque glass doors and gestured toward a pair of white leather sofas facing a massive glass desk. The large room was empty.

Clayton sat first, maintaining the silence even after the secretary departed. Like Johnson, his gaze swept the space, eventually settling on the vast collection of framed photographs behind Livia Castellan's desk. Each one was carefully placed along a sleek mantle, deliberate and precise.

The soft click of a door to their left pulled them away from the collage.

"I see you've taken an interest in my family."

The woman's hair was stark white, yet nothing in her face betrayed her age. Livia Castellan wasn't tall, but her posture, presence, and confidence made her seem far younger than her years.

Clayton was the first to rise. "Mrs. Castellan, I'm Detective Muttler, and this is my partner, Detective Johnson." He extended a hand, feeling an odd urge to address her as he might a man. She was feminine and graceful, yet there was something in her eyes—something sharp and unyielding. This was a woman who had worked hard for everything she had.

She was shorter than most, but her perfectly tailored pantsuit gave her an air of authority, making her seem taller than she was.

Livia Castellan moved toward her chair, pausing briefly to adjust one of the framed photographs. Then, with a quiet sigh, she settled behind the desk, her eyes locking onto Clayton.

"It's been years since anyone called me Mrs. Castellan, Mr. Muttler." She leaned forward, linking her fingers together. "I haven't had a husband in ages. Ms. Castellan will do just fine. Now, what can I do for you gentlemen?"

She held their gazes, unwavering.

Johnson didn't hesitate. "Murder, Ms. Castellan." He remained seated, his tone flat.

Clayton caught the flicker of tension in her knuckles as her fingers tightened. Her expression stayed calm, but anger rippled beneath the surface.

She stared at Johnson in silence for several seconds before responding. Then, with a smile, she leaned back in her chair.

"Ah, yes. The two strangled girls. But what does that have to do with me?"

Clayton felt his pulse quicken, but he remained still, leaning back into the sofa as he waited for Johnson's response.

"Orbis Noir is your company, Ms. Castellan. So is Anonyme. Both victims used your service."

She shrugged, unfazed. "Two unlucky women who could have just as easily used another service and met the same fate."

Johnson shook his head. "So you're telling me that two women were murdered after being whisked away in cars your company provided, and you have no concerns? You don't see a connection?"

Clayton stepped in. "What my partner is saying, Ms. Castellan, is that it's unusual. Both victims used your service. It could be that another client—or someone with access to the drivers—might be our killer. Maybe even someone working for you. That's what we're here to find out."

Livia's green eyes remained fixed on Johnson. "I run a business, Mr. Muttler. That is all. That is my job. Your job is to solve those murders."

Johnson stroked his chin with thick fingers. "Do you have kids, Ms. Castellan?"

"I've had four husbands and several children, Mr. Johnson—one of whom never made it to his ninth birthday." Her brows knitted together, and for a moment, her chair seemed to swivel toward the mantle behind her. But she stopped herself.

"My sons are my only joy," she said, motioning to the office around her. "All this comes second to them. But as long as I am alive, I am the matriarch. I am the boss." She paused, shaking her head. "I always wanted sons—never daughters. A woman knows things, and I knew I could never abide having daughters. I would have expected too much from them...but as fate had it, I did have a daughter. She is also dead."

She seemed to catch herself, shifting her gaze to Clayton. "Again, I ask—what is the purpose of your visit?"

Clayton held her gaze, the warrant securely in his pocket. "We need access to the victims' profiles, as well as the locations where your vehicles dropped them off."

"We wanna know if they even made their appointments at all," Johnson added, leaning in close. He held her gaze, the faintest hint of a grin at the corner of his lips. "And we need a list of your clients for the last six months."

Clayton observed the tension as Johnson and Livia Castellan locked eyes. It was clear neither of them liked the other.

THE TWO DETECTIVES MADE NO COMMENT AS THEY EXITED ORBIS NOIR. Clayton could hardly wait to leave the building, and as soon as they hit the parking lot, the words slipped out.

"She knew we were coming."

Johnson nodded as he slid into the driver's seat. "And she damn well knew we had a warrant, too."

Clayton slammed the passenger door shut as he squeezed into his seat. "Did you hear what she said about the victims?"

Johnson cranked the engine and slapped the steering wheel. "She knew they were strangled. That ain't public information. So how the hell did she know?"

Clayton let out a shocked laugh. "Someone from the precinct tipped her off. That's how."

Johnson pulled out of the parking lot and sped east on Dominion Street. "I get the feeling there's a lot more going on with this case than we know."

"Why would anyone want to warn Livia Castellan we were coming?" Clayton asked, his voice laced with confusion.

Johnson's foot was heavy on the gas. "Let's ask Mitchell Milan," he said. "I know he told someone something. The guy's cars picked up both victims, for God's sake!"

"Fine, let's head over there now. We've gotta pick up that GPS info on the cars anyway." Clayton tapped the envelope on his lap, containing the details Livia Castellan's company was obligated to provide. "We've got the list of clients for the last six months. We just need to look for patterns—see who's using Anonyme the most."

Johnson's erratic driving soon took them out of the city, and as the sedan wound its way toward Westbridge Executive Transport, Clayton admired the water below the cliff. In the distance, Kingsley Docks came into view, with the small silhouette of the warehouse containing all those expensive cars. The scenery was peaceful, almost serene. Clayton smiled as birds soared above the water on their left.

As they crossed the bridge, Clayton decided to dive into the contents of the envelope. He tore open the seal just as Johnson flicked on the radio and began humming to a song he obviously liked.

Then came the deafening pop of a tire exploding.

Clayton's heart leapt into his throat as the car jerked violently to one side. The world seemed to slow as the vehicle swerved uncontrollably, the sound of screeching rubber and metal clashing filling the air. His hands gripped the seat as he braced for impact.

A second loud pop, sharper this time, and the rear window behind him shattered with a sickening crash. Glass rained down on him, a sharp sting across his face, but it was nothing compared to the raw panic flooding his chest. The car lurched, swerving dangerously close to the bridge's rails.

"Someone's fucking shooting at us!" Johnson's voice snapped him out of his daze, but the panic in the air was suffocating. Clayton could barely hear Johnson over the ringing in his ears. The road blurred as they veered closer to the edge.

Time seemed to stretch, and Clayton's body was frozen, as if his brain hadn't caught up to the danger yet. A cold sweat drenched his palms, and his stomach twisted. The roar of his heartbeat was deafening in his ears.

Instinct finally kicked in, and Clayton shoved the envelope deep into his shirt, his movements frantic as the car skidded closer to the guardrails. His mind was racing, but it felt as if he were moving in slow motion. The sound of the tires screaming against the pavement drowned out all else as the car veered toward the edge of the bridge, threatening to send them crashing into the water below.

Clayton's breath caught in his throat as the vehicle made contact with the rail—everything blurred, and then, the world tilted. The car plummeted. His mind went blank from the shock, the cold weight of fear sinking deep into his bones. But one thing was clear: the envelope was still tucked tightly inside his shirt.

30

Dominion General Hospital was only a few blocks from Orbis Noir, where Clayton and Johnson had been just hours earlier. Now, late in the evening, Clayton lay stiffly on a hospital bed that was far too small for his tall frame. Every shift sent a dull ache through his muscles, and the stinging cuts on his face reminded him of the shattered glass from the crash. His shoulder throbbed, but other than that, he figured he'd be okay.

Johnson, sitting up in the bed beside him, had a bandage over his right brow. He exhaled sharply, shaking his head. "I had that damn car for years," he muttered bitterly. "At least another five left in it."

Clayton let out a slow breath, his head pounding. "I'm just thankful we're alive." He dropped his head forward, trying to ease the pressure in his skull.

The door creaked open, and both men looked up as a nurse walked in.

Johnson's grin spread wide. "Hey, babe." He turned to Clayton, eyes gleaming with mischief.

The nurse shot him a sharp look, crossing her arms. "Don't you smile at me, Rodney." Her voice was firm, but there was something in her expression—something between exasperation and amusement. "You scared the hell out of me."

"Ah, I'll be fine." Johnson waved a dismissive hand before turning to Clayton. "Meet the missus—Lina. Babe, this is Clay Muttler." He reclined comfortably as Lina adjusted his pillow. "Ain't it sweet having your wife work at the hospital you're in, kid?"

"Keep that up, and I'll make sure you stay here a couple extra days," Lina shot back. "Maybe I'll finally get some peace and quiet at home."

"Oh, come on, babe!" Johnson groaned.

Lina rolled her eyes before shifting her gaze to Clayton. "You think he's annoying at work?" She laughed playfully. "Try living with him—he's twice as crazy."

Her grey eyes shimmered with warmth, and Clayton found himself momentarily caught by the way they seemed to glow. Lina was petite, wore little makeup, and carried herself with an easy confidence. She moved closer, examining the cuts along the side of his face.

"These shouldn't take long to heal."

Lina gave her husband a lingering look before heading for the door. "I'll check in on you boys later."

"We don't plan on being here too long," Johnson said.

"I can't stay here much longer," Clayton added. His voice was quieter, more distant. The sterile smell of antiseptic clung to the air, and memories pressed in—his mother, the long hours spent by her hospital bed, the slow fading of her presence. That weight settled in his chest, mixing with the raw frustration of being trapped here after someone had just tried to kill them.

He clenched his jaw. There was a murderer out there, and someone wanted him and Johnson dead. Lying in this bed wasn't going to get him any closer to the truth.

"You think those gunshots had anything to do with our two murders?" Johnson asked, his voice low but firm. "I've solved a few high-profile cases in my day. Put guys behind bars for life. But this?" He exhaled sharply. "I'm sure being shot at has everything to do with Evelyn Greene and Sabine Aldrich."

Clayton nodded, wincing as pain flared in his neck. "Your driving saved us back there, Johnson." His mind drifted back to the crash—the sickening impact, the rush of icy water, the struggle to force the doors open. They had barely managed to shatter the windows and fight their way to the surface.

"Had to be quick," Johnson replied, as if shaking off the weight of what had happened.

Clayton's gaze shifted to his clothes draped over the chair beside his bed. His eyes locked onto the wet envelope resting next to them, the paper warped from the water but still intact. He exhaled, his jaw tightening. "You think this has anything to do with our visit with Livia Castellan?"

THEY WERE CLEARED TO LEAVE THE HOSPITAL LATE IN THE EVENING, AND Clayton could hardly wait to get home. The day had been long, chaotic, and far from uneventful.

He stood beside Johnson and Lina, with their boss, Wade Dawson, positioned between them. Dawson's sharp eyes scrutinized both men, though it was clear—despite his tough exterior—that he cared.

"You two better get some rest tonight," Dawson said, his voice firm but carrying an undertone of concern. "You've got work to do tomorrow."

Clayton nodded, catching the paternal look in Dawson's eyes. He'd heard whispers around the precinct—Dawson's wife had died a few years back. Cancer. A part of him wondered if the man had any kids.

Lina leaned into Johnson, squeezing his arm as she turned to Dawson. "Don't worry about him. I'll have him out the door on time in the morning."

Dawson smirked. "I don't doubt it, Lina. You keep this one in line."

Johnson exhaled, rubbing the bandage over his brow. "I just can't believe we lost a whole damn day."

Clayton shook his head, waving the still-damp envelope in front of Johnson's face. "All is not lost. I gotta go over this before I turn in tonight," he said. "Didn't have a chance to look at it all day."

Johnson pointed a finger at him, eyes narrowing. "Hey, aren't we supposed to go through that together?"

"You can see it all tomorrow, Rodney." Lina cut in before Clayton could respond. "We're going home. And you better find yourself a new car first thing in the morning, because I'm not driving you to work."

Clayton grinned at Johnson while Dawson watched the exchange in silence. "Don't worry, buddy, I'll pick you up bright and early." He reached out to slap Johnson's shoulder—just as a familiar voice cut through the air.

"Clayton Muttler!"

Everyone turned just in time to see Aunt Ruby striding toward them, her face a mix of fear and fury.

"I oughta slap you silly, boy! You nearly died today, and you didn't have the gall to call and tell me?"

Clayton barely had time to react before she wrapped him in a fierce hug. Over her shoulder, his eyes met Dawson's. His boss just shrugged, and in that moment, Clayton realized—Aunt Ruby was his emergency contact. Who else could he have listed? She was the only family he had.

And yet, as that thought settled, the image of Elijah Brooks flashed through his mind. His father. His blood. But never his family.

Aunt Ruby finally pulled back and turned to Dawson. "Thank you for reaching out, Mr. Dawson." She shot Clayton a pointed glare. "At least I know someone's got an eye on this one."

Clayton winced. "Aunt Ruby, you know I was gonna call you when I got home."

She scoffed, already walking away. "When you got home? Boy, you know that ain't good enough. Now, get moving. I'm driving you home."

Clayton sighed but didn't argue. He simply waved the wet envelope at the others before following her to the car.

31

A hot shower was all Clayton needed the moment he got home. He let the water cascade over him, hoping to wash away the horror of the day—the gunshots, the shattering window, the sickening drop in his stomach as the car plunged over the bridge and into the water. But no matter how long he stood there, the memories clung to him like damp clothes.

Afterward, he tried to eat, but his appetite was gone. Someone had tried to kill him. That wasn't something he could brush off.

This was his first case as a detective—his first as lead, and he wasn't about to fail. A murderer was still out there. And Clayton could feel it in his bones—someone, whether the killer himself or another player in the game, wanted him and Johnson off this case.

CLAYTON SETTLED INTO BED, AS COMFORTABLE AS HE COULD BE AFTER THE day he'd had. He reached for the envelope Livia Castellan had been forced to hand over, running his fingers over the damp edges. A small smile tugged at his lips—strange how a simple warrant, just ink on paper, could strip power from someone like her.

But he had seen the look in Castellan's eyes. She wasn't afraid.

Livia Castellan understood the game, the laws, the loopholes. Maybe she wasn't a murderer, but Clayton had no doubt she'd do whatever it took to protect her company.

As Clayton leafed through the damp pages, smudged ink blurring in places, he focused on the details of Evelyn Greene's and Sabine Aldrich's profiles. Both women had created their accounts on Anonyme just days before their deaths—first-time users.

A few pages in, something else stood out. The victims had been driven to different locations. That meant no clear pattern, no obvious link in where they had gone. He and Johnson would need to check both places themselves.

He exhaled, letting the weight of the case settle over him. Two women had signed up for a night of fun, but instead, they had ended up dead. And now, staring at their profiles, Clayton could only draw one conclusion —someone was using Anonyme to hunt.

But why them? What was it about these women that had made the killer choose them?

He shifted in bed, his joints aching from the crash, a dull reminder of how close he and Johnson had come to dying. Clayton exhaled sharply, wincing as he adjusted his position. Exhaustion pulled at him, but something in those damp pages refused to let him sleep.

He rubbed his eyes, pressing his fingers against the bridge of his nose. Think. The victims weren't random. The killer had chosen them for a reason. But why? And how?

He tried to conjure a profile, piecing together fragments of intuition and what little evidence they had. Does he live alone? Maybe. A loner. Someone who doesn't draw attention. Or does he fall into the other category—the regular guy? The kind who blends in, who has a wife, a house, a couple of kids, even a dog?

Clayton frowned, staring at the ceiling. No... He didn't believe this was just some guy playing pretend at normal life. The killings felt controlled, precise. Not random.

He was certain of one thing. The killer was a man.

And right now, that man was still out there, watching, waiting for his next victim.

He turned another page, his eyes scanning the damp ink smudged across several columns of names—the Anonyme client list from the past few months. Some names were redacted, black bars swallowing identities in a way that made Clayton's gut tighten.

Then, his gaze snagged on a name that shouldn't have been there.

Elijah Brooks.

His chest tightened. For a moment, the sound of the city outside faded into nothing.

Elijah Brooks.

His fingers pressed into the paper as if his grip alone could erase the name. He blinked, forcing himself to read it again, making sure his mind wasn't playing tricks on him.

But it was there, plain as day.

Elijah Brooks.

His father, the mayor.

The man he'd only learned about after his mother died a year ago. The man he had no childhood memories of, no connection to beyond a name and a hollow space where a father should have been.

Clayton sat up, his exhaustion fading away. His heart slammed against his ribs. He had spoken to Elijah Brooks twice in his life—two strained, uncomfortable conversations that left more questions than answers.

And now his name was in front of him, tangled up in a murder case.

His fingers tightened around the paper. He felt the damp edges crumpling beneath his grip.

What the hell was he doing on Anonyme?

Coincidence?

Clayton didn't believe in coincidence.

32

Clayton gripped the wheel tighter as he drove toward the precinct, his thoughts circling. He had no clue how to proceed. How the hell was he supposed to move forward with the case knowing the city's mayor—his father—was a client of Anonyme?

His jaw clenched. For all he knew, Elijah Brooks had tipped Livia Castellan off, giving her just enough time to prepare. But why? And why wasn't his name redacted like the others?

Was it a slip-up? Or a message?

A muscle in his temple pulsed as he exhaled through his nose. Maybe Brooks wasn't high-profile enough to earn Castellan's protection. Or maybe someone wanted Clayton to find his father's name. But apart from his aunt Ruby, no one else even knew about their connection.

And now that secret was sitting in plain sight.

Either way, it changed everything.

Pulling into the precinct parking lot, Clayton killed the engine and let his head drop against the steering wheel. His body ached, his mind felt like static. He had forgotten to pick up Johnson.

Shit.

He was about to restart the car when a sharp rap against the window made him flinch. His breath caught, heart slamming into his ribs as the terrors of the previous day came rushing back—the gunshots, the shattering glass, the sickening plunge into the water.

His fingers twitched toward his holster before he forced himself to breathe. It was just a knock. Just a knock.

But for one awful second, it hadn't felt like one.

Clayton found himself staring into familiar green eyes—sharp, curious. He couldn't forget those eyes, nor the pale skin, the tight afro, or the way Elliot Frost always carried Blackwing 602 pencils like a writer from another era.

The reporter grinned, and Clayton, despite himself, returned it as he stepped out of the Range Rover.

"Hello, Clay."

Frost's handshake was firm—too firm. A sharp jolt of pain shot through Clayton's fingers, setting off a chain reaction of aches from his bruised body. The plunge into the water replayed in his mind in a flash: the impact, the struggle, the cold pressing in.

"I heard about your accident," Frost said, his tone as smooth as ever, but his eyes sharp with interest.

Clayton nodded, but before he could even form the question in his mind, Frost was already answering it.

"A car going over the only bridge leading to Kingsley Docks? That's no secret, Clay."

Clayton exhaled through his nose, wagging a finger at him. "You got something there, man."

Frost gave a half-smile, then tilted his head. "How are you feeling?" His tone was sincere.

Clayton moved gingerly toward the precinct. "Could be worse," he admitted.

There was something about Frost that put him at ease, despite only having met him once. Maybe it was the way the reporter cut through the usual bullshit, or maybe it was how he reminded Clayton of the friendships he'd let slip away. His mother's illness had reshaped his world, pushing everything else—everyone else—aside. By the time he had the space to look up again, most of those friendships had faded into the distance.

Frost cleared his throat. "Look, I'll get to the point." His green eyes flicked left, then right, but when they landed back on Clayton, they didn't waver. "I've been looking into these girls—the ones who got murdered. And a few others who went missing."

He pulled a notepad from his bag, flipping it open. "Girls no one would miss—at least, that's what the bastard who took them probably thought. But they all had families. They all had someone who cared."

Clayton's intrigue sharpened. "What've you got?"

Frost pressed his thick red lips together before speaking. "A couple months ago, a girl was found buried in the middle of nowhere." He ran a thumb over the edge of his notepad. "But nothing stays hidden forever. Eventually, everything comes out."

Clayton felt his jaw tighten, his mind flashing to the name he'd seen hours ago. Elijah Brooks. Some things came out. Others stayed buried.

"What're you saying, Elliot?"

Frost tapped his Blackwing 602 against the page, his voice quieter but edged with certainty. "She was found way outside this city's jurisdiction. But I think she was killed by the same person who murdered your two victims."

A chill threaded through Clayton's spine. A pattern. A history.

He needed to hear more.

33

Rodney Johnson sat at his desk with a stack of papers scattered in front of him. His mind was flooded with memories of the accident the previous day, and every muscle in his body ached. Glancing up at the empty desk across from him, Rodney understood his partner's tardiness—especially since Muttler hadn't even called that morning to offer that ride to work. He was much older than Muttler, but Rodney knew what the kid must have been feeling; they had both been in that car when it skidded off the bridge and into the water. They were there together when the gunshots rang out—when the violent crash of his prized car shattered the day.

Johnson had faced plenty of physical encounters with perps in his time, but he'd never been the target of an assassin's gun.

He rubbed his temples and took a deep breath, knowing that if Muttler was feeling even half as bad as he did, the kid was having a damned rough time. This was a hell of a way for a rookie detective to start his first case—his first real lead.

But Rodney knew the kid was tough. Muttler would pull through. They both had to.

Familiar footsteps reached his ears, and Rodney looked up to see Muttler striding toward his desk. The kid looked like hell—bruises along his jaw, dark circles under his eyes, and a stiffness in his movements that said he felt every inch of yesterday's disaster.

Clayton dropped a stack of case files on his desk, then slid a coffee across to Johnson—an extra large, his unspoken apology for not picking him up.

Johnson gripped the hot drink eagerly and nodded. "Lina had an early start. Dropped me off here at five." He took a long gulp before setting the cup down on top of the scattered case files.

Clayton cringed at the organized mess on his partner's desk, but that was just Johnson—he'd never change.

As Clayton arranged the files on his desk, he could feel Johnson's eyes on him.

His partner grinned and took another gulp of coffee. "So, tell me, kid. Did you have someone over nursing you back to health last night, huh? Was it our good mayor's assistant—what's her name again..." He scratched his chin, snapping his fingers. "Uh... Ellis... Naomi Ellis. That's it!"

Clayton felt his face flush. Was it that obvious how he felt about Naomi? He cleared his throat, steering the conversation back to business.

"Uh, speaking of the mayor," Clayton said, forcing his voice to stay neutral. "Guess whose name showed up on Anonyme's client list?"

He slid a crumpled envelope across Johnson's messy desk—the same one that had gone over the bridge with them in the crash.

Johnson whistled as he scanned the pages. "I can't wait to see the look on Dawson's face when he finds out."

Clayton shook his head. "Dawson won't find out. Not yet."

Johnson's eyes met his. "Hey, you sure about this, kid? This'll piss Dawson right off—not to mention yours truly."

"We keep this to ourselves," Clayton said. "Dawson will get over it... he'll understand."

He took the sheet bearing his father's name and locked it inside his desk before producing another—a copy he'd made himself with Elijah Brooks's name redacted. He wouldn't tell Johnson why he'd really been late. He couldn't mention that he'd trusted Elliot Frost enough to share what he'd found, trading secrets in exchange for everything Frost had on an entirely different case in another town. And he definitely couldn't mention that the reporter had been the one to make that copy, erasing the mayor's name from the list.

Clayton hated keeping things from Johnson, but he had to do this his way.

Johnson's brows furrowed in thought. "I see. From the way Castellan was acting, you think someone at the precinct—or even Brooks himself—is feeding her information. But why? Why is Castellan mixed up in all of this?"

Clayton leaned in across the desk. "Wait'll you hear what else I've got to tell you, Johnson."

He saw it in Johnson's eyes—he had his full attention.

"Evelyn Greene and Sabine Aldrich may not be the killer's first victims."

Johnson placed his coffee on the desk. "Keep talking."

"I met with that reporter from the press conference the other day, and—"

Johnson cut in. "The funny-looking white guy?"

Clayton shook his head. "No, he's a Black man with albinism."

Johnson shrugged. "The guy's whiter than I am, kid."

"And that makes him unique," Clayton said. "Let's get back to what Frost told me. Nearly an hour's drive from here, there's been a whole slew of missing girls— all matching the descriptions of our two victims. Thing is, they've found one... buried out in a field."

Johnson brought his hand to his lips. "No fucking way."

"Yeah, that's another thing we need to check out," Clayton said.

Before either could say more, their conversation was interrupted by a colleague—Varendra from ballistics.

VARENDRA WAS YOUNG, BUT SOMETHING ABOUT THE WAY HE MOVED AND spoke made Clayton think of an old soul. He couldn't have been much older than thirty, yet his dark eyes carried the weight of experience. He was South Asian, with wavy, shoulder-length hair that framed his sharp features.

After a nod to the detectives, Varendra opened a file folder. "We examined the shell casing from the tire. Your shooter used a Remington MSR."

Clayton's body tensed, a shiver creeping up his spine at the thought that the second bullet could have struck him in the back of the head. He looked at Varendra with interest. "Isn't that a manually operated bolt-action piece with a rotary locking bolt?"

Johnson let out a loud laugh. "Well, what do you know, the kid knows his guns."

Varendra didn't so much as grin. He simply nodded, his gaze steady on Clayton. "Whoever shot at you either got this off the black market or has plenty of money—these rifles run around fifteen grand."

Clayton and Johnson exchanged glances, both knowing exactly what the other was thinking. Only one name came to Clayton's mind.

Livia Castellan.

The head of Orbis Noir. The owner of Anonyme.

34

There was plenty to do, but Clayton had no intention of skipping his lunch appointment with Elliot Frost. Just after noon, he left the precinct and walked north toward a shopping plaza a few blocks away.

Once again, he hadn't told Johnson where he was going or who he was meeting. He had told him everything Frost had shared about the missing girl who had turned up dead. Like Evelyn Greene and Sabine Aldrich, Paige Whitmore had a spouse. But unlike the victims in Clayton's case, Paige had never used Anonyme.

Clayton spotted Elliot Frost the moment he stepped into the food court. The guy was hard to miss. As he reached the table, he couldn't help but notice the Blackwing 602 tucked into Elliot's blond afro, just above his left ear. Left-handed.

They bumped fists in greeting and got straight to business.

Elliot's green eyes sparkled with mischief. "So, how'd your partner take the news about us scratching each other's backs?" His question came with a childlike chuckle.

Clayton grimaced. "Johnson knows you gave me the details, but not about our arrangement. That said, he's no fool—I'm sure he'll figure it out." He exhaled, still carrying a trace of guilt. They had nearly been killed together, for God's sake. Shaking off the thought, he added, "We're heading out tomorrow to talk to the detective—about Paige Whitmore."

Elliot tapped his pale fingers on the table. "Any chance I can tag along?"

Clayton nodded. "Sure. It'll give Johnson a chance to get to know you."

Elliot didn't miss a beat. "Now, about Mayor Brooks." His tone sharpened, shifting gears like a true reporter. "I'll keep my word and hold onto what you told me about him being a client of Anonyme. But what do you plan on doing with that information?"

Clayton met those intense green eyes. A part of him wanted to unload everything—to let go of the weight—to tell Frost that Elijah Brooks wasn't just a name on a list. He was his father.

But his gut told him to hold onto that truth a little longer.

His mother's dying wish had been clear: Find your father. Tell him you exist.

That conversation had to happen between him and Elijah Brooks—alone.

Clayton and Frost continued their discussion over lunch. On the way back to the precinct, Clayton couldn't help but wonder what they'd learn about Paige Whitmore the next day. Would her cause of death mirror the others? Would they find any connection to the same killer?

He'd just have to wait and see.

UPON HIS RETURN, CLAYTON FOUND JOHNSON WRAPPED UP IN BUSINESS OF his own. His partner was practically glowing—his new Dodge Durango had just been delivered to the precinct.

Johnson dangled the keys in front of Clayton. "Feel like going for another ride, kid? We need to check out those Anonyme spots—the ones where Evelyn and Sabine had their appointments."

Clayton nodded. "Since you're so excited about your new ride, you can drive us to Stonebrook tomorrow. We've got a meeting with Detective Blaides."

ELLIOT FROST SAT ALONE IN HIS CAR, PARKED IN A NEAR-EMPTY LOT. HE'D made a point of arriving long before Clay and his partner, Rodney Johnson, were due at the Stonebrook precinct. In his line of work, being on time wasn't enough—he had to be ahead of the game.

Besides, a guy like him had to work twice as hard to build a solid reputation.

Elliot had made plenty of sacrifices to earn his place at The Sentinel Review, but there was one line he never crossed: he wouldn't betray a source just to get first dibs on a story. He did honest work and kept his promises.

He took in Stonebrook's skyline—few high-rises, an overwhelming number of historic homes, and sprawling gated communities. It was an old town, rich with history, and like any other, full of both good and bad.

Elliot pulled his Blackwing 602 from his afro and tapped it against his knee, his thoughts circling back to Paige Whitmore—the first found in a string of missing women.

A black Dodge Durango rolled up beside him. He tucked the pencil back into his hair and grinned when he saw Clay in the passenger seat.

35

Clayton sat across from Detective Blaides's desk, listening intently as the middle-aged man spoke about Paige Whitmore. Beside him, Johnson and Frost remained just as silent, absorbing every detail. It was crucial to learn as much as they could.

The Stonebrook precinct was small, and it didn't take long for Clayton to notice the lack of resources he often took for granted. Outdated equipment, aging technology—even the police cruisers looked like relics. But none of it seemed to slow Blaides down. The man's dedication to his job was evident.

Blaides was older than Johnson, though Clayton couldn't tell by how much. His salt-and-pepper hair was the thickest Clayton had ever seen, and his deep voice carried a quiet authority. He was tall—but not taller than Clayton.

Clayton listened as Blaides spoke, the steady scratch of Frost's Blackwing 602 filling the brief pauses in conversation.

When Clayton met Blaides's gaze, he saw history—a man shaped by both solved and unsolved cases. His experience was evident, but there was no arrogance in him, no trace of cockiness—just a detective who had seen it all and kept going.

"Paige didn't have an easy life," Blaides said, his tone carrying the weight of someone who knew her personally. "Nothing came easy for her. But she worked hard to put her life back together—moved back home with her mother, got clean, left the streets behind."

Clayton and Johnson exchanged glances as Frost's note taking picked up speed. Clayton already sensed what Blaides was about to say, and from the look in Johnson's eyes, so did he.

Blaides leaned forward, locking eyes with Clayton, then Johnson. He barely acknowledged Frost, despite the reporter being the one who had arranged the meeting. "Every last one of those missing girls were prostitutes. But that doesn't mean they deserved to be murdered. It doesn't mean nobody cared about them."

"What can you tell us about the body?" Clayton asked. He needed the photos. The autopsy report. He needed to see for himself.

CLAYTON LAID THE FILE OPEN ON THE DESK, A MISSING PERSON'S PHOTO IN HIS hand. Paige Whitmore had been a pretty girl, and the fact that someone had decided to cut her life short was an atrocity. But he had to look into those eyes—see her as she was before it happened.

He felt Johnson over his shoulder and heard the quiet scratch of Frost's Blackwing 602.

Clayton studied Paige's face, committing it to memory before he turned the page. He already knew what was coming next.

The first few images took Clayton's breath away and filled him with anger toward the man capable of such a thing. Paige's body was in an advanced stage of decomposition, and the report stated she had likely been dead for several weeks before she was discovered.

"The poor girl." Frost stood to Clayton's right, his voice barely above a whisper.

"Look here." Johnson held the coroner's report in his hand. "Says she was strangled." He flipped through the pages, scanning them quickly.

Clayton knew exactly what his partner was searching for. "What does it say, Johnson?"

Johnson shook the report as he handed it over. "It confirms what we suspected. This girl was strangled." He reached for one of the photos, tapping a specific area. "Check this out. The bruising is faint, but it lines up with the report. The killer used something to strangle her."

Clayton nodded. "And we have a pretty good hunch about what he used."

Blaides looked at them, puzzled. "You think it's the same unsub?"

Johnson nodded, casting a quick glance at Frost, as if he still wasn't completely sure about trusting the reporter. "Son of a bitch uses silk..."

This was a crucial detail Clayton had never shared with Frost. He glanced at the reporter, catching those intense green eyes fixed on him, but he wasn't concerned. Not anymore.

They had already explained the killer's method of staging his victims to Blaides and Frost, but suddenly, a realization struck Clayton like a bolt of lightning. His pulse quickened. He couldn't contain it.

"The missing girls—even Paige. They meant nothing to him—at least, not the way the others did."

Blaides' brows furrowed, his eyes darkening. "What the hell are you getting at?"

Clayton stepped closer, lowering his voice, keeping it calm and measured. "I'm trying to get inside this guy's head—think the way he does. Look at the pattern. He staged the last two victims. Almost like he's entered a new phase. Like he's evolving."

Johnson whistled, pointing a finger at Clayton while Frost scribbled furiously in his notepad. "I see where you're going with this, kid. The missing girls were practice runs. They were important, but only enough to get him to the next level. No makeup, no airbrush, no staging. He picked victims he knew no one would go looking for. Prostitutes."

Clayton snapped his fingers, nodding. "Exactly." He scratched his chin, deep in thought. "This guy's been at it for a long time—at least more than three years."

Johnson exhaled sharply, fury flashing in his eyes. "Now we just need to find out who the fuck he is."

36

They had parted ways with Elliot Frost after leaving Stonebrook and made their way to the two venues used by Anonyme. Now, as they drove back, Clayton reclined in the passenger seat of Johnson's new Dodge Durango, eyes closed, letting the hum of the engine and the soft strains of the radio lull him into a brief escape. Beside him, Johnson hummed along to his favourite tunes, fingers tapping idly on the wheel.

But Clayton's mind refused to settle. It was cluttered with the case—flashes of crime scene photos, fragments of conversations—and the trauma of the past few days. If luck hadn't been on their side, he and Johnson would be in the morgue right now.

His thoughts drifted to his mother, and an unshakable question took root: what really happens after death? Would he see her again? He clenched his fists, forcing himself to push those thoughts aside. He had no room for his own mortality—not now.

Johnson turned off the radio, and Clayton knew he was ready to talk.

"So, you think our guy did the same sick thing to Paige Whitmore as he did to Evelyn and Sabine?" Johnson's voice was tight, the words catching in his throat. Clayton didn't need to wonder why.

Keeping his eyes closed, Clayton exhaled. "If that's his MO, I'd say he did the same."

Johnson's large palm slapped the steering wheel. "But why rape them after he kills them, huh?"

"I can't answer that," Clayton admitted. "But according to the reports, there was no bruising or healing response—a dead body doesn't react to trauma the same way a living one does. So, we know the assaults were post-mortem." He opened his eyes, blinking into the sunlight. "It makes sense that all his victims would suffer the same fate."

Johnson grunted but said nothing else. They drove in silence for nearly ten minutes, both lost in thought, the weight of what these women had endured pressing down on them.

Finally, Clayton spoke, knowing Johnson would welcome the shift. "Those places were spotless. Livia Castellan isn't stupid; I'm sure they were scrubbed top to bottom. I'd be shocked if we found a single print between the two spots."

Johnson nodded. "But damn, were they upscale. We're talking serious money. Sliding walls, upstairs bedrooms—the whole works. They even had bars."

Clayton had seen it all. He sighed. "Those suites make regular apartments look like squalor. And for what? One night of luxury."

Johnson chuckled. "Unless you're the mayor." He leaned forward as he laughed, the Durango swerving briefly into the next lane before he corrected it. "Talk about a repeat customer, kid! Brooks must've used that service at least ten times. Did you see the number next to his name? You'd think the guy didn't have a wife at home."

Clayton said nothing. He didn't want to think about it.

AFTER ANOTHER LONG, GRUELLING DAY, CLAYTON ARRIVED HOME WELL PAST 8

PM. He'd already showered and wanted nothing more than to sink into the couch with a bowl of Grape-Nuts ice cream—his favourite.

Soft melodies from Radio Paradise filled the room, but Clayton wasn't listening. His mind was elsewhere. On one name.

Elijah Brooks.

Johnson's words had echoed in his head all day. The mayor—his father—had used Anonyme. Multiple times. What did that mean?

And then there was his mother's dying wish. *Find your father. Tell him you exist.*

He scooped another spoonful of ice cream, letting it melt on his tongue. The cold didn't soothe him. Instead, he felt like he was disappearing piece by piece, weighed down by the case and the nagging truth that his father was out there. Within reach.

He wanted it all to go away.

But deep down, Clayton knew it was time.

The ice cream sat forgotten in his lap as an overwhelming feeling washed over him—like his mother was right there in the room, nudging him toward what he'd been avoiding.

It was time to face the man who made him.

37

The next morning, Clayton drove straight to Civic Tower. As he stepped inside the building, a heavy sigh escaped him. He had no clear plan—just a reckless determination that could very well cost him the case. Maybe even his job.

But he had to move forward. With this. With everything.

The page from Anonyme, bearing his father's name, was tucked safely in his pocket. He felt its weight like a brand against his skin.

At the elevator, he pressed the button, ignoring the sudden tightness in his stomach. The moment the doors slid shut, his mouth went dry. His pulse drummed in his ears. Still, he took a steadying breath. *Keep going.*

When the elevator doors opened, Clayton stepped out, his eyes locking onto the set of double doors at the end of the hall. The gleaming nameplate was impossible to ignore.

Elijah Brooks.

Then, a soft voice cut through his tunnel vision.

"Clay?"

Naomi Ellis.

She was already rising from her desk, moving toward him, puzzled. She knew exactly where he was headed.

As she reached him, he placed a gentle hand on her arm. "Let it go, Naomi," he murmured.

For a split second, his eyes softened—she had that effect on him.

"I'll explain later," was all he said.

Naomi hesitated, searching his face. Then, with a small nod, she let him pass.

Elijah Brooks sat behind his desk, phone pressed to his ear, engaged in his usual morning call with his wife when the doors to his office burst open.

His gaze snapped up, startled—but years of discipline kept his expression unreadable. He remained still, his posture composed, betraying nothing.

Muttler.

Elijah didn't move, didn't speak. He simply watched as the young detective stormed into his office, radiating defiance.

The boy was trying to prove himself. That much was clear. Perhaps he wanted to make a name for himself, to show the world he was fearless. But that didn't excuse his insolence.

One look into Muttler's eyes told Elijah that he'd expected something else—rage, indignation, maybe even a show of power. But Elijah denied him the satisfaction.

He remained seated, silent, and unmoved.

And in that silence, Muttler had already lost.

The moment of truth had arrived, yet Clayton stood before his father, frozen. His feet felt anchored to the ground, his mind scrambling for the right words.

Across the desk, Elijah Brooks sat motionless, watching. Waiting.

The silence stretched between them, thick and suffocating.

Then, Clayton thought of his mother. The woman who had been his everything—his protector, his comfort, his only parent. Memories of her voice, the lullabies she'd sung, the way she'd fought to give him a good life—all of it swelled inside him. *Mona Muttler was my mother and my father.*

The surge of emotion broke the dam.

"Johnson and I were almost killed the other day." His voice was steady, sharp. "Do you have anything to say about that, *Mister Mayor*?"

He stepped forward, slamming the Anonyme list onto the massive desk. *Lead with the truth.* That had been his plan. Force this man to see him for who he was—his own flesh and blood.

But standing here, staring into the eyes of Elijah Brooks, Clayton realized something unsettling.

This was the second hardest thing he'd ever done.

The first was watching his mother's coffin disappear into the ground.

And now, here he was—facing the only blood relative he had left in the world. A man he couldn't even decide if he hated.

Clayton kept his gaze fixed on his father as his eyes swept over the list of names. The longer he watched him, the angrier he became. His father shrugged, nonchalant, as though his actions meant nothing.

"So, my name's on a list," his father said. "For all I know, someone could've put it there just to make my life difficult." He almost smiled at Clayton, proud and cocky. "Is this why you barged in here like you own the place?"

"I came here because you're a monster!" Finally, the words escaped, and Clayton began to feel the weight of a burden he'd carried for a year start to lift. He needed to keep talking—to release whatever it was his mother had left with him.

His father gazed at him, puzzled, but Clayton saw it: Elijah Brooks was finally seeing him.

"You were probably around fifteen or sixteen. My mother was fourteen." Clayton's fists clenched tighter.

"Mona Castillo—Castillo was her father's family name." She was just fourteen years old, and you raped her.

Recognition flickered in his father's eyes. But still, he sat silent. Speechless.

"Mona Muttler." Clayton blurted his mother's name. "That was my mother—the woman you left pregnant, then walked away, building your life while she was left behind!" Clayton's body shook, uncontrollable. His voice cracked, but he couldn't stop. He wanted to call him every name in the book—mayor, father, and worse.

"Do you know what it's like for a kid to come home from school and only have a few minutes with his mother before she left for the night shift, even after working all day? Do you know how it felt for a six-year-old boy to be left alone at night while his mother worked to make ends meet? She was a kid herself, and you left her with a baby. And because she refused to give me up, her parents threw her out..."

Clayton had to pause to catch his breath. He brought his hand to his face, realizing it was wet with tears. He wept for his mother. Clayton wept for the man before him, whom he hardly knew. He wept because he suddenly felt free of the burden his mother had passed to him. And in all his weeping, he wondered how she had carried it for so long. She was stronger than him. That was his mother. That was Mona Muttler.

He turned to walk out of the office, and saw Naomi standing by the open door, her mouth slightly ajar.

Clayton passed her without a word. He couldn't look her in the eyes.

PART III

38

It was impossible to control himself. Impossible to stop.

Here, in his own space, no one could find him. No one knew who he really was.

He cleaned the Remington with methodical precision, but the weapon blurred in his unblinking gaze. He was a good shot, but he'd failed. That detective was still alive.

He ran the cloth over the barrel again. He'd polished the Remington MSR so many times since missing, as if he could wipe away the mistake itself—the unbearable fact that he had missed. But deep down, he knew the truth. He despised guns. They were crude, impersonal. He preferred to take life with his hands.

Detective Muttler.

Detective Clayton Muttler.

The name alone stoked the fire inside him. He wanted to watch the life drain from the detective's eyes. To feel the fight leave his body. But no. That would ruin everything. A kill like that—impulsive, messy—would defile the craft he'd worked so hard to perfect.

There was no satisfaction in that. No artistry.

What he needed was vengeance.

He needed to teach the detective a lesson.
He just wanted to be left alone.

39

Johnson sat at his desk, watching Muttler as they reviewed the details of their case. The kid had been distant these past few days, and Johnson didn't feel it was his place to ask why.

Muttler had shown up late the other day without so much as an explanation, and from the look of him, Johnson could tell it had nothing to do with their case—or at least, he hoped it didn't.

They had spent the morning going over what they knew so far. A serial killer, one who not only strangled women but also knew his way around assault weapons.

Johnson scratched his chin, still eyeing Muttler as he considered a new possibility—was the strangler working alone, or did he have an accomplice? His lips parted to voice the thought, but Muttler seemed lost in another world.

TWO DAYS AND COUNTING.

Clayton rubbed the side of his head, trying to shove the memories of the past forty-eight hours to the back of his mind. But the words he had spewed in his father's office kept circling back. He had never expected to break down—never thought it would be so hard to say what had been festering inside him for so long. The truth was, he still didn't know what he felt. Or what he was supposed to feel.

Johnson's silence said it all. He knew something was off. And Clayton couldn't decide what to do about it—what to say about what had gone down at the Civic Tower.

They had a case to solve. A killer to catch. But Clayton couldn't shake the nagging suspicion that his father was somehow connected to it all, no matter how minor that involvement might be.

When he had confronted Elijah Brooks, what had he really expected? And now, after everything, why did the silence feel worse? His father hadn't reached out. Not a call. Not a word. He had spent his whole life without a father, yet ever since the truth had come to light, some part of him had wanted to know this man. Maybe even be accepted by him. Maybe even... loved.

The thought filled Clayton with frustration. He shoved the papers away, shoving the emotions with them, and stood abruptly, avoiding Johnson's eyes.

Then he turned toward the door—and froze.

Across the floor, at the far end of the room, a man stood watching him.

Elijah Brooks.

His father.

40

Clayton did as he was told.

He followed the mayor into the elevator, but not before glancing back at Johnson's puzzled, angry eyes. His partner thought he was holding out on him.

Father and son left the precinct together—the elder taking the lead, dictating where their conversation would take place. Clayton trailed behind, his movements automatic, his thoughts a tangled mess. He felt numb. Blank.

Several blocks later, he found himself on a park bench, the weight of silence settling between them. His father had spoken only once—to tell him to follow.

And Clayton had obeyed.

He sat with his elbows on his knees, staring at the grass beneath his shoes, but Clayton could feel his father's eyes on him.

"None of it happened the way you think it did."

Those were his father's first words.

Clayton lifted his head, forcing himself to meet those eyes. "Are you calling my mother a liar, too?"

His father exhaled sharply, shaking his head, his broad shoulders rising and falling with frustration. "It wasn't like that. Mona couldn't have—"

"No." Clayton's voice was a low snarl. "You don't get to say her name. Not in my presence."

His father's nostrils flared—a flicker of the effort it took to maintain the calm that seemed to come so easily to him. "Look, son—"

"I'm not your son." Clayton's tone was steel. "You don't get to say that either."

A long sigh. Then, finally, his father spoke again. "We were kids. I remember Mo—your mother well. She was a nice girl. We went on our first date. Her friend set it all up."

Clayton said nothing, holding his father's gaze. He needed to hear this. He needed something beyond what his mother's letter had given him.

"Neither of us had any experience," his father went on. "Hell, I was nearly sixteen and had no clue about sex or what could happen if things went all the way." He paused, exhaling slowly, as though unburdening himself.

"Look, kid. I know you don't like me." His voice steadied, finding its resolve. "I could see it in your eyes the first day we met. And I won't pretend to be a good man—I can be a real son of a bitch. A real bastard. But I'll tell you this." He met Clayton's eyes again. "I didn't force myself on your mother. We just... got to a place where she got scared and wanted to stop. And I was at that place where I didn't know how to stop."

Clayton felt his stomach tighten.

His father glanced toward the empty swings in the distance. "I left her that night not knowing what had really happened. Not knowing that you had happened. And even if I had—if she'd found me, told me she was pregnant... What the hell could I have done? My father would've killed me."

Clayton swallowed hard, his mother's letter surfacing in his mind. He had read it over and over, dissected every word.

And never once had she written the word *rape*.

His father's voice dragged him from his thoughts again.

"Like it or not, you're my son. I won't just disappear now that I know you exist."

Elijah Brooks stood, dusting off his hands as if brushing away the weight of the conversation.

But Clayton wasn't letting him off that easily.

He rose to his feet, towering over his father. "These murders—do you have a hand in them?" He didn't wait for an answer. "I won't back down, no matter how deep you're in. If it comes to it, I'll slap the cuffs on you myself."

His father scoffed and walked away, shoulders set, back straight—unshaken. Yet his words carried over his shoulder, deliberate and firm.

"You have two brothers and a sister. Family."

A pause.

"The ball's in your court."

Clayton closed his eyes, inhaling slowly. Holding it. Feeling the weight of it all settle in his chest.

Then, he exhaled.

41

He returned to his desk after wandering the park alone, sinking into his chair just as Johnson's glare landed on him—silent but heavy with unspoken frustration.

Clayton knew he owed his partner an explanation. He had to give him something. But how much of his personal life should he share? How much of it was tangled in this case, now that his father's name sat in the middle of Anonyme's list of clients?

It was rare to see Johnson this quiet, this brooding. And Clayton knew why. The misunderstanding. The fact that Johnson had no idea what was really going on.

Clayton glanced at his partner—a man he respected, not just as a colleague but maybe even as a friend. Then, he made his decision.

"Hey, Johnson."

His partner's eyes flicked up, wary. "Yup?"

Clayton grabbed his coat. "Let's get a coffee."

Clayton and Johnson sat on the same park bench where he'd been with his father earlier. He'd told Johnson everything—his connection to the mayor, the truth he'd been carrying for a year.

His partner took a long gulp of coffee, letting it all sink in.

Clayton's eyes were fixed on the swings in the distance. He'd wanted Johnson to hear it from him first—before the rest of the precinct inevitably found out. "So, what's your take on all this mess?"

He turned to Johnson, expecting some insight, but all he got was the same stunned look his partner had worn since he broke the news.

"Did that damn reporter know before I did?" Johnson spat, his tone sharp with irritation. He valued loyalty.

"You're kidding, right?" Clayton shook his head. "Frost never knew then, and he doesn't know now." Johnson scoffed. "You may not like the guy, but he's one of the good ones. And I trust him."

A slow grin crept across Johnson's face. "But not enough to tell him before me, huh?"

"Johnson, you're such an ass."

"Fucking right," Johnson said, shaking his head. "I'd have been damned jealous if you trusted Elliot Frost over me." His brows lifted, still in disbelief. "So, all this time—even when we walked into his office at Civic Tower—you knew?"

Clayton sighed. "Like I said, I found out a year ago when my mother died. I knew who he was, but that was the first time I met him in person."

Johnson let out a low hiss. "Dawson's gonna lose his shit—his golden boy, the mayor's son."

"You can't talk about this, Johnson. Not yet."

His partner grinned wide. "Just remember me when you take Dawson's job, kid. I'm sure your pops will hook you up."

Clayton pointed at him. "You know it won't be like that."

Johnson chuckled. "Oh yeah? In case you haven't noticed, Brooks is a family man. I'll give him that."

He finished off his coffee, crumpling the cup before tossing it in the trash. Then, he slapped his hands together and stood. "Come on, kid. Time to revisit that lovely spot where we nearly got murdered."

Clayton nodded. Their case was moving forward—but not fast enough. Johnson was convinced they might have missed something at the crime scene.

Clayton hoped he was right.

Because they needed a break. Something. Anything.

They needed to find the man who nearly killed them.

And the man who was still out there strangling women.

They were almost certain it was one and the same.

42

Naomi Ellis sat at her desk, staring at the mayor's office door.

Her family had known Elijah Brooks for as long as she could remember. She had him to thank for her job. But as she sat there, she found herself wondering—did she really know him at all?

She hadn't spoken a word about what had transpired in that office the other day. Not to her father. Not to anyone.

Clayton's voice echoed in her mind, the weight of his words pressing against her chest. Could the man she had grown up believing was a good and honourable leader—the man who was like a brother to her father—really be everything Clayton said he was?

Her gaze drifted to the nameplate on the double doors across the room.

Elijah Brooks.

Clayton Muttler's father.

The same Elijah Brooks whose name was on a client list for Anonyme—the same service that might be tied to Evelyn Greene's death.

A knot formed in her stomach.

She reached for her phone, hesitating. She wanted to call Clayton. Needed to. But was it the right thing to do?

Mr. Brooks had always been clear: office business was confidential. And the fact that he had a son—one no one knew about—was the kind of secret she should never repeat.

But that didn't mean she couldn't talk to Clayton.

She sighed, running a finger over the strap of her purse.

She could still feel the warmth of Clayton's hand on her arm, the gentle but firm way he had held her, even in his anger. The sensation sent a shiver down her spine—something she could barely explain, let alone admit.

Naomi glanced at the clock, then stood.

She grabbed her purse and headed for the door.

Back at the precinct, Clayton stayed late to meet with CSI Lyle Chamney about the shell casings they'd found near the bridge at Kingsley Docks.

Johnson's hunch had paid off. The two had walked the length of the bridge, carefully tracing the shooter's likely position. It was Johnson who spotted the casings first, half-buried in the dirt near the railing—Remington MSR rounds, just like the ones that nearly killed them.

Now, in the harsh glow of the evidence room lights, Clayton studied the two new pieces of evidence through their sealed bags. He exhaled. "If this guy's our strangler, he really screwed up leaving these behind."

Chamney took the bags with gloved hands, tilting them slightly under the light. "Wouldn't be the first time someone got sloppy. And who knows? Maybe he thought we'd never come back."

Johnson folded his arms. "Doubt we'll find prints. He's too careful for that."

Chamney smirked. "Oh, you'd be surprised what a little black powder or cyanoacrylate fuming can pull up, dear Rodney."

Johnson rolled his eyes. "One of these days, Chamney, you'll call me by my first name, and I won't know what to do with myself."

Chamney chuckled as he started toward the elevator, holding up the evidence bags like a prize. "I'll have something for you two in the morning. Until then, try not to get shot at again, hmm?"

Clayton watched him go, feeling the faintest smirk tug at his lips. Chamney was one of the best—always had been. His knowledge went beyond forensics, stretching into cars, technology, even aircraft. If there was a way to find something on those casings, Chamney would do it.

The elevator doors slid open, and just as Chamney stepped inside, a familiar figure passed him by, walking straight toward Clayton.

Naomi Ellis.

Clayton inhaled sharply, caught off guard. She was here—at the precinct, after hours, moving with purpose. Her expression was unreadable, but the way she was looking at him told him one thing.

She had something to say.

It had been a simple discussion over dinner—fast food, eaten in his car with the case files spread between them. They'd talked about his father, about the investigation, and everything in between. Clayton had glanced at the time, knowing he should call it a night, yet here he was, driving Naomi home, not ready for the evening to end.

Now, standing at the entrance to her building, he felt something shift. The night air was cool against his skin, but there was warmth between them—a quiet pull, unspoken but undeniable. Naomi turned to him, her keys in hand, her gaze searching his.

"You want to come up?"

A simple question, but it sent his heart into a sprint. He should say no. He should be thinking about the case, about the killer still out there, about the tangled mess his life had become. But all he could focus on was the way she was looking at him, like maybe she felt the pull too.

His jaw tensed. "Naomi..."

She smiled—soft, understanding. "Just for a little while?"

Clayton exhaled slowly. He wasn't sure if crossing this line was a mistake, but in that moment, he didn't care.

"Yeah," he said. "Just for a little while."

43

Clayton drove to the precinct after dropping Naomi off at Civic Tower, the silence of the morning filled with memories of the night before. The warmth of her embrace, the taste of her kiss, the way her fingertips traced along his skin—it lingered, making the world outside feel distant.

He hadn't made it home. Instead, he'd showered at Naomi's, her scent clinging to him, her presence still wrapped around him like a second skin. She'd even made him breakfast—something simple, but somehow, it had felt like more.

Now, parked outside the precinct, he sat in his Range Rover for ten extra minutes, holding onto the night a little longer. Holding onto her.

For once, there was no case, no killer, no questions running through his mind.

Just Naomi.

Just this.

And for now, that was enough.

Inside the precinct, Clayton walked to his desk, fully aware that Johnson's sharp eyes would piece everything together before he even sat down.

Sure enough, as he pulled out his chair, his partner's banter began.

"Well, well, look who got lucky last night!" Johnson grinned, rising to his feet. "Go on, tell good old Rodney all about it."

Clayton waved him off, fighting to keep his smile in check. "Lay off, Johnson."

But Johnson wasn't about to let it go. "Oh, I know what you did last night, kid." He gestured toward Clayton's clothes. "Same outfit as yesterday —first time I've ever seen that." He sniffed the air dramatically. "And what's that? Jasmine? That ain't your shower gel, Muttler."

Clayton shook his head, letting out a quiet laugh, embarrassed but undeniably happy.

44

He'd spent most of the day taking target shots—anything to make sure he wouldn't miss next time. His lair was safe, secluded. No one could find him there. No one could hear the gunfire.

Still, he needed something to keep his hands busy—something to steady his nerves. His gaze swept across the workroom, landing on his gear—his colours, the airbrush. The bolt of silk. It had been too long.

But he'd promised to wait.

Jaw tightening, he clenched a fist and pressed it against his temple, forcing the urge back down.

Finally, his thoughts settled on the one obstacle standing in his way.

Clayton Muttler.

He moved to the window, gazing out into the moonlit night. Silence stretched across the landscape, broken only by the steady beat of his own pulse.

Stepping back, he turned to his workspace. Everything was in its place—meticulously arranged, waiting. His instruments beckoned, whispering to him, calling his name. They longed for his touch. But he only ever reached for them when he needed them... when it was time to create.

The urge swelled inside him. Too intense. Too consuming.

His eyes shifted to the door, locking onto the keys hanging from the hook on the wall.

Red Fern Row was new to her, but the work wasn't.

Lexx had recently moved to Stonebrook, drawn by its quiet streets—a stark contrast to the chaos of city life. No more fighting for clients. No more arrests. No more judgment for being who she was.

She had stayed out later than usual that night, her heels clicking against the cracked sidewalks of the dimly lit stretch on the outskirts of downtown. Compared to where she came from, Stonebrook was just a tiny place lost in a big world.

She took slow, deliberate steps—movements she had practiced for years. But turning tricks had never been her dream. Lexx had ambitions. But sometimes, life had a way of shoving you down paths you never planned to take.

The boarded-up shops and cheap motels whispered stories no one cared to tell. The air was thick with gasoline and desperation, a perfect mix for Red Fern Row's clientele.

When the truck pulled up beside her and the headlights flickered, Lexx knew it was time to work. Her last trick of the night. She just hoped this one understood—she never went farther than oral. That was the rule. Her only rule.

45

It was just after 1:00 AM. Most of Stonebrook lay in darkness. His truck sped northward, the illuminated road ahead the only thing his widened eyes could see. Beyond that, there was nothing. No plan. No destination.

Why had he left his lair? Why had he broken his promise after working so hard to suppress the urge?

Avoiding the rearview mirror, he stole a quick glance behind him. The imposter writhed on the back seat—hands bound, mouth gagged, eyes wide with fear. They had seen his face.

And for that, they had to die.

His grip tightened on the wheel. Everything was ruined.

Now, he was just driving. Dawn would break soon, and he had no idea what to do.

The thought made him cringe, his pulse quickening as the memory replayed in his mind.

How could he not have known?

How could he not see he was being fooled?

46

Clayton lay in Naomi's bed, staring across the dimly lit room. The air was thick with her scent, surrounding him, calming him. The weight of her head on his chest was comforting, anchoring him in a moment he didn't want to end.

They lay in silence, wrapped in each other's warmth, neither willing to break the spell.

Finally, he pressed a kiss to the crown of her head. "I could do this every day."

Her lips brushed against his chest, sending a shiver through him. Then came her soft laughter, light and teasing.

"Careful what you wish for, Clay."

The sound consumed him.

But as he sank deeper into her presence, his thoughts betrayed him, drifting back to Civic Tower. Back to the man who had upended his life.

His father.

"You have two brothers and a sister. Family. The ball's in your court."

Elijah Brooks was waiting. Expecting Clayton to come to him.

Naomi's nails traced gently across his skin. "You've gone quiet again." Her voice was low, knowing. "You're thinking about him."

Clayton exhaled, surprised at how well she could read him. "And why do you say that, princess?"

She lifted her head, meeting his gaze. "I can feel it. The way your body tenses. The way your silence screams at me."

"Naomi..." He sighed, running a hand down his face.

But she pressed her palm to his chest, easing him back against the pillows. "No, you listen to me. I've known Elijah Brooks since I was a kid. He's not perfect—no one is."

"Come on, Naomi, do we have to talk about this now?" He shut his eyes, hoping she'd drop it.

She didn't.

"You want to go to him." It wasn't a question. "I can feel that too. But Clay, if you're waiting for Elijah to come to you, it's not going to happen."

"I just don't know." He tugged at his goatee. "There's this curiosity... this need to know him. But I can't let him in."

"Let it flow." She kissed him, soft, lingering. "Let go of your pride. Meet him halfway."

He ignored that.

"And then there's this case." He exhaled sharply, mind shifting. "What the hell do I do if I find out he's tied to all of this? Johnson and I nearly died."

Naomi didn't hesitate. "Elijah Brooks is a lot of things, Clay. But he's no killer."

Something flickered in her eyes. A thought brewing.

Clayton caught it instantly. "What's going on?"

"You say Anonyme is the key to solving this case, right?"

He sat up slightly. "Yeah. Why?"

"Elijah got an invitation yesterday." Naomi bit her lip. "Livia Castellan is hosting a birthday party this weekend. At her mansion."

Clayton leaned forward. "Can you get us in?"

Naomi slipped out of bed, her naked curves making him briefly reconsider every responsibility in his life. She smirked as she reached for her robe.

"Is the sky blue?"

CLAYTON WAS RUNNING LATE AGAIN—BUT NAOMI WAS WORTH IT.

He pulled the Range Rover up near the entrance of Civic Tower, her hand resting in his. Their goodbye kiss was brief but lingering, cut short by the sudden buzz of his phone.

Clayton glanced at the screen. "It's Johnson. Work."

Naomi smirked as she reached for the door handle. "Pretty soon, he's going to hate me."

"Impossible." Clayton's voice was soft, certain. "How could anyone hate you, princess?"

She gave him one last playful look before stepping out, disappearing into the building as he answered the call.

"Yeah, Johnson, I know—I'm running late."

"Like you've been late every morning this week, kid." Johnson's voice was laced with amusement.

Clayton chuckled. "I'm on my way to the precinct now."

Johnson's tone shifted, the humour fading. "No, you're not. Frost was here waiting for you when I got in. He and I are heading to Stonebrook now. Meet us at the precinct there. Blaides has another body, and he's keeping the crime scene locked down until we get there."

47

The drive to Stonebrook felt much longer than the first time he'd visited, but as Clayton arrived at the scene, he spotted Johnson and Frost standing with Detective Blaides. Several cruisers were parked in front of the police tape, their blue and red lights flashing.

His first observation? Stonebrook police had little experience in securing a crime scene. There were just too many people beyond the tape, and Clayton hissed, shaking his head.

He hurried over to where Johnson and Frost stood with Blaides, his words aimed at Stonebrook's detective. "You've got too many people past the tape."

Blaides glared at him, his eyes hard. "I trust my people."

Clayton blinked slowly, tilting his head. "But—"

Johnson cut him off with a pat on the shoulder. "Save it, kid. You won't get anywhere with this one, take it from me."

Frost's green eyes darted from side to side, his face barely suppressing a grin. As he pulled his Blackwing 602 from his blonde afro, the reporter greeted Clayton with a nod. "This one seems different."

Blaides snapped his fingers, and two constables quickly moved aside as he led Clayton and Johnson toward the victim.

Noticing Frost wasn't following, Clayton glanced over his shoulder at the reporter.

Frost tucked his Blackwing 602 back into his blonde afro and shrugged. "I think I'm good right here for now," he said, biting his thick red lips slightly.

As Clayton approached the body, he realized why Frost had decided not to take a second look. The reporter was right.

This one was different.

CLAYTON AND JOHNSON STOOD WITH BLAIDES, ALL THREE OF THEM GAZING at the corpse. Something was different this time—something felt off. But Clayton couldn't quite put his finger on it.

The girl lay in a patch of bushes, but it was clear whoever left her there had no intention of hiding the body.

"The killer was in a hurry," Clayton said, crouching to examine the boot prints near the body.

"You really think so, kid?" Johnson knelt beside him.

"I'm almost positive." Clayton's eyes scanned the victim, pausing at her neck. "She was strangled—same MO as the others. But why just drop her like this?" He pointed to a smudged patch of makeup near her jaw. "See that? He started working on her. Started using his airbrush."

Johnson exhaled sharply. "Yeah, you're right, kid. Same guy."

Clayton stood and turned to Blaides. "We need everything we can on her. Get photos before anyone moves the body. No one touches her until we've got what we need."

Blaides hesitated, his jaw tightening as though irritated by the command. Then, with a slow nod, he forced a smile. "Anything else, My Lord?" His voice dripped with sarcasm.

Johnson got to his feet, still staring down at the girl. "I think our guy messed up. We need to sweep the area—see if he left anything behind."

Clayton pulled out his phone and stepped away from the scene. He needed help with this one. And he knew exactly who to call.

Clayton stood near the entrance of the Stonebrook precinct, arms crossed, his eyes scanning the street. It had been hours since Blaides finally opened the scene, allowing the girl's body to be removed, but there was still plenty of work to do before they could leave Stonebrook.

Beside him, Johnson let out a chuckle, shaking his head. "Kid, you're full of surprises, you know that?" He nudged Clayton with his shoulder. "First, you drop the biggest bomb that you're Brooks's son, and now I find out you can just pick up the phone and summon a top-tier criminal psychologist like it's nothing? Who the hell is Sable Crowder?"

Clayton smirked, glancing at his partner. "She was my professor back in college. I took a couple of her classes, and she helped me through some rough times."

Johnson raised a brow. "Ah, that explains how you always seem to get inside this guy's head."

"Doesn't mean I'm right," Clayton said. "That's why I called Sable."

At that moment, a sleek black sedan pulled up to the curb. The door opened, and a tall woman stepped out, her presence commanding yet effortless.

Clayton's eyes brightened. "Here she comes now."

As Sable approached, Clayton couldn't help but smile. She hadn't aged a day. For a woman in her late forties, Sable Crowder carried herself with the confidence and vibrance of someone a decade younger—calm, composed, effortlessly charismatic.

She swept her black hair away from her dark eyes before pulling him into a warm embrace. "How's my favourite student?"

Clayton chuckled. "I thought you were still upset I didn't follow in your footsteps."

Sable gave him a knowing look, as if reading his soul. "You're still young. There's time."

Before Clayton could introduce them, she turned to Johnson, offering her hand with an easy smile. "Sable Crowder."

Johnson hesitated, clearly caught off guard. Clayton knew exactly what was going through his partner's head—Sable had that effect on men, without even trying.

"Rodney Johnson," he finally managed, still holding her hand a moment longer than necessary.

Sable turned back to Clayton with a smirk. "Well, young man, let's hope this was worth the long drive." She started toward the precinct doors, her presence commanding without effort. "You're lucky Charlie isn't the kind of husband to curtail my comings and goings."

Clayton laughed, following her inside. "I couldn't see any man having that kind of control over you, Sable."

48

Clayton and Johnson sat across from Sable Crowder in a cramped, dimly lit room. The small window let in barely any light, and the flickering overhead fixture did little to help. It was all Detective Blaides had offered them. The Stonebrook precinct was small, and with another murder shaking the town, chaos filled the halls.

"Let's make this quick, Clay," Sable said, leaning back in her chair. "I've got a teenager at home who's been texting me nonstop since before I even got here."

Clayton sifted through his memory, forcing himself to bring the crime scene back into focus. Blaides had provided photos, but the image of the victim's lifeless body was already burned into his mind.

"Our guy was in a hurry," Clayton murmured, flipping through the pictures. "I just don't get why he dumped her like this. It's sloppy."

"Have they identified the victim?" Sable asked, absentmindedly twirling a lock of her dark hair around her finger.

Johnson had his palms pressed against the table. "Doesn't seem like she'd been living in Stonebrook long," he said. "I heard Blaides telling one of his guys she might've been working Red Fern Row." He gave them both a knowing look. "You know what that means."

Clayton nodded. Red Fern Row had a reputation.

"He did start to paint her," Sable said, her voice thoughtful. "But you told me he only used some girls as practice for his real masterpieces. Something changed. Something went wrong." She squinted slightly, her dark eyes partially veiled. "Serial killers take breaks. It could be days, months—even years. What if he'd decided to stop killing?"

Clayton leaned forward, locking eyes with Sable. From the corner of his vision, he could see Johnson watching, listening intently.

"But maybe he couldn't stop," Clayton said. "The urge was too much. Normally, he wouldn't waste his best work on a girl like our victim, but he had no choice..."

"You mean he needed a fix?" Johnson asked, scratching his chin.

"Something like that," Sable replied.

Clayton exhaled, running a hand over his jaw. "If this guy was the one who shot at us, maybe he feels we're getting too close. Something about us working the case pushed him."

"What if we're closer than we think?" Johnson muttered.

Sable was about to speak when the door swung open. Blaides stood in the entrance, his expression unreadable. He lingered a moment before finally saying, "I think our coroner just found something you all need to see."

Clayton sprang from his chair, adrenaline spiking. Something in Blaides's eyes told him this was big.

"Where are we going?" he asked.

"To the morgue," Blaides said. "Don't worry, it's right next door."

As Clayton stood over the naked body of the latest Stonebrook victim, he noted that Elliot Frost was nowhere to be seen. The reporter was damned good at his job, but he couldn't stomach sights like this—the raw violence, the aftermath of pain.

The coroner, an older man with weary eyes, remained silent, letting Clayton, Sable, Johnson, and Blaides make sense of what lay before them.

Clayton's mind worked quickly, piecing together the what and the why. The killer had been spooked. And the evidence was right there in front of them.

Johnson let out a low whistle—for the fifth time. "Talk about convincing." He shook his head. "This shit is getting weirder by the minute."

Blaides stood by, saying little, but his eyes were sharp. He was waiting to hear what Sable had to say.

"You were right, Clay," Sable said, stepping closer. "Now we know why your unsub ended his work abruptly and discarded this poor soul the way he did."

Clayton's gaze remained fixed on the victim. His eyes drifted to the left, where a brown lace-front wig lay beside the victim's shaved head. "Any idea who he is?" His gaze moved downward—to the stab wounds in the groin.

Blaides shook his head. "We're working on trying to find where he lived. But he was definitely new to Stonebrook.

"Poor fella," Johnson muttered. "Had no idea what the hell he was walking into."

"The killer was caught off guard," Sable said, studying the scene. "It's safe to say he was fooled. He thought he was picking up a woman—his next masterpiece."

Clayton nodded. "But look at what he did once he realized the truth." He motioned toward the wounds to the victim's groin. "There's barely any bleeding. Hardly any blood on the clothing. I think he stabbed him after he was already dead—maybe hours later."

"Which means," Sable added, "he found out after he'd already received... some kind of service. Before he was ready to paint his masterpiece."

"But he stopped short." Clayton moved closer to the body, glancing at the coroner. "Hey, have you checked his mouth?"

The coroner looked puzzled. "What for?"

Johnson scoffed, shaking his head. "DNA evidence."

Sable's brows lifted in thought. "The other victims showed signs of post-mortem sexual assault. You think he planned the same for this one?"

Clayton nodded. "He was angry. He felt betrayed—tricked. And that's probably because of what happened right before the rage set in."

Johnson exhaled sharply. "Oh, shit... she went down on him... then he found out she was really a he."

A tense silence filled the room as the coroner pried open the victim's mouth with gloved hands. The look he gave them said it all.

Clayton's hunch had been right.

PART IV

49

Clayton and Johnson sat at their desks, combing through the details of the case. Thanks to CODIS, they had now confirmed that Evelyn Greene, Sabine Aldrich, and the latest Stonebrook victim—now identified as Lexx—were all murdered by the same killer.

Johnson exhaled, shoving a stack of papers and photos aside. "So, we know the guy who killed Evelyn and Sabine is the same one responsible for the murders in Stonebrook. And like you said, those killings were just practice runs." He raked a hand through his thick hair. "But there's no trace of him in CODIS. And that print we pulled from the shell casing? Nothing in AFIS either."

Clayton nodded. "He's been careful for a long time. But he's slipping. Losing control."

Johnson scratched his chin. "You think someone's protecting him?" His voice was low, but Clayton could hear the hesitation in his tone—like he wasn't sure he wanted the answer.

"The mayor, you mean?" Clayton tilted his head, half-smirking. "Don't worry, Johnson. If my old man is involved in this in any way, he'll pay for it. I already made that clear to him."

Johnson gave a noncommittal shrug.

Clayton met his gaze, firm. "Now do you get why I don't want this thing between Brooks and me coming out just yet?" He leaned back, a thought coming to him. "By the way, get your best threads ready, partner. Livia Castellan's birthday party is tomorrow, and we've got invitations."

Johnson groaned. "It's all Lina's been yapping about since I told her. She wants to come. Told her it's not happening."

Clayton smirked but didn't reply. His thoughts drifted to Naomi—he could hardly wait to see her later. As the mayor's assistant, she was expected to be at the Castellan mansion.

50

The drive to the Castellan mansion was scenic, the countryside stretching out on either side of the road. Clayton admired the rolling hills in the warm glow of early evening, the sky ahead burning red as the sun inched toward the horizon. The hills felt like they were closing in around him—just like the mysteries of the case, just like the weight of the strange, tangled dynamic between him and his father, the mayor.

A gentle touch on his thigh pulled him from his thoughts. Clayton glanced over, his tense expression easing into a smile. Naomi was beside him, her presence grounding him in the moment. She looked radiant in the dimming light, her black beaded dress catching every flicker of movement, sending tiny sparks of reflected gold dancing across her skin.

She smiled knowingly. "He knows you're coming, you know," she said, shifting in her seat. "I had to tell him I invited you."

Clayton shrugged, eyes flicking back to the road. It was as if she could read his mind. "I'm not going for him, Naomi." His hands tightened on the steering wheel. "Johnson and I are looking for a lead—anything that might help us crack this case." Then, he glanced at her again, a softer note slipping into his voice. "And you, of course."

Naomi studied him for a moment before speaking. "What do you expect to find at Livia Castellan's birthday party? You think the killer is just going to walk in and announce himself?"

Clayton smirked. "No, sunshine." He stole another quick glance at her. "But that doesn't mean he won't be there. My gut tells me the killer is connected to Anonyme—maybe a client, maybe an employee. I think he's closer than we realize."

"Then let me help you, Clay." Naomi leaned in closer, her hand sliding up his thigh.

Clayton chuckled, gripping the wheel a little tighter. "Careful what you're doing, sunshine... Trying to drive here." He shot her a sideways glance. "And don't think I don't know what you're up to. I don't want you anywhere near this case. Johnson and I already got shot at, remember?"

"All I need to do is create a profile—become a client." She squeezed his thigh again, her voice smooth, persuasive.

"You're asking me to use you as bait. Not gonna happen." His voice was firm, but he knew Naomi wasn't the type to let things go.

Thankfully, the Castellan mansion came into view, bringing an end to the conversation—at least for now. He'd told Naomi a dozen times before: what she was suggesting was out of the question.

The Range Rover rolled past towering iron gates bearing the words *Castellan Manor* and an elaborate family crest. A valet gestured toward the parking area, where an array of luxury cars gleamed beneath the estate's golden lights.

Clayton stepped out and rounded the vehicle, offering his hand to Naomi. But before taking it, he paused, his gaze lifting to take in the massive structure before them.

Night was falling quickly, but the mansion blazed with light. The air buzzed with excitement as guests in evening wear filed toward the grand entrance.

As Clayton took Naomi's hand and started toward the estate, they stopped short at the sight of two familiar figures approaching.

Johnson whistled low, his eyes sweeping over Naomi with an appreciative grin. "Well, aren't you a sight for sore eyes, pretty lady."

He nudged Elliot Frost in the ribs. "Yeah, kid, the reporter's my plus one."

Frost chuckled. "Clay, this one's a real piece of work." He greeted Naomi with a quick kiss on the cheek before heading toward the entrance.

Clayton hung back with Johnson, watching the pair ahead of them.

Johnson smirked, nudging Clayton. "You know, the reporter ain't all that bad. Got a killer sense of humour."

Clayton shook his head, laughing. "Yeah, yeah."

Inside the massive hall of Castellan Manor, Clayton stood with Johnson and Elliot Frost, the albino reporter, as they took in the extravagance of Livia Castellan's birthday celebration. So far, he hadn't seen the powerful business mogul herself, but he had spotted Elijah Brooks the moment he walked in—his father, the city's mayor, standing alongside Naomi.

Clayton could hardly take his eyes off them. Naomi was right there, close to his father, her posture relaxed, her expression open. He watched them for a while, studying the ease between them, the effortless way they communicated, the laughter they shared. A strange weight settled in his chest. He shook his head, as if trying to rid himself of unwelcome thoughts.

Johnson moved in closer, his deep voice low. "I've yet to see the belle of this expensive ball," he muttered. "Where do you think she's hiding, kid?"

Clayton smirked. "Don't worry, Johnson. Livia Castellan is here. From what I remember, she likes to make an entrance."

"Oh yeah." Johnson nodded. "Like that time in her office—one second, nothing. Next second—poof! There she was."

Frost, standing to Clayton's right, rubbed his pale hands together. "I did a piece on her once for The Sentinel Review—even got to interview her. That story changed my career. Put me where I am now."

Johnson chuckled. "Maybe that's why you got an invitation. Castellan probably wants another glowing article."

Frost tilted his head slightly. "Oh, I'll write a story, alright. But I get the feeling she won't like this one."

Johnson scanned the opulent hall. "How old do you think the queen of the manor is, anyway?"

Clayton shrugged. "Women like her don't usually like to reveal their age."

"That was the one question she refused to answer when I met her," Frost said. "Believe me, I pressed." His face softened a little. "Not that I blame her. Why should it matter? A man in her position never gets asked, even when he looks a hundred years old. Livia Castellan takes care of herself. Gotta give her that."

Johnson grunted. "Yeah, but she ain't young, either."

LIVIA SAT AT HER DRESSING TABLE, GAZING INTO A GILDED MIRROR NEARLY AS wide as the wall. A slow smile threatened to surface as she recalled where she had first seen it—an opulent estate in France, a lifetime ago. She hardly remembered the owner's name; it didn't matter. What mattered was that she wanted the mirror. So she made an offer. Livia always got what she wanted.

Age had been kind to her—or rather, she had forced it to be. Healthy living and discipline played their part, but the real credit went to the finest cosmetic surgeons money could buy. And yet, birthdays disgusted her. She would never stop the passage of time, but she could make sure no one ever saw it touch her.

The faint sound of music drifted in from the great hall. Her guests were waiting. But Livia was a deliberate woman. She did things when she was ready, and others would wait—even her children. They knew better than to step into that hall without her. And yet, one of them, the thorn in her side, had yet to come home. She'd told him not to be late.

Her gaze shifted to the wall beside her, where a collection of gilded frames hung in perfect symmetry. Her children.

She lingered on her daughter's portrait. Lana. Gone too young. But for that, Livia was grateful. The girl had been soft, and softness had no place in a world built for men.

Her sons, though—they were her joy. Her legacy. They would shape the future.

Except one.

Livia's expression hardened as her eyes landed on a single portrait.

She should have let him go the same way as Lana.

But she hadn't. And now... now, she wasn't sure which was worse.

Pushing the thought aside, she rose from the bench, smoothing the silk of her gown. It was time to greet her guests.

51

Clayton did his best to look beyond the ice sculptures, the endless trays of caviar, and the never-ending flow of champagne and wine. His gaze moved from face to face in the great hall, wondering if one of them belonged to a killer.

He'd seen his father with a beautiful woman—his wife, obviously—but had done his best to avoid crossing paths with him. He was here for a lead in the case, not a family reunion. Their eyes had met briefly across the room, but Clayton had given nothing in return. Not even a nod.

A light touch on his arm. Naomi.

He turned to her and offered a strained smile. "Someone in this room could very well be the murderer."

Johnson, standing close by, overheard. "And it's the same bastard who nearly killed us." He exhaled slowly. "I've been staring into every pair of eyes, looking for someone who feels... off. Nothing."

Clayton chuckled. "He's not gonna offer a friendly greeting, Johnson."

Naomi stepped closer, and the scent of her perfume momentarily pulled him from his thoughts. "Apparently, Livia is waiting to make her grand entrance with all her sons—except one of them is late."

Johnson huffed. "Ain't that always the case with kids?"

Frost stood beside Naomi, his black suit making his pale skin stand out even more. "All I can say is, she loves her sons."

"And she made sure none of them have anything to do with the business," Naomi added. "They're all grown, but Livia dotes on them. They travel, they party, they spend her money."

Frost grinned. "Not necessarily in that order. Castellan was married four times. But get this—when I interviewed her, I found out not all her sons are actually Castellans. Only the two youngest: Gabriel and Adrian. Identical twins. Gabriel died when he was nine."

Clayton met Frost's green eyes with interest. "She did mention she was married a few times, right, Johnson?"

"Something like that." Johnson was still scanning the crowd. "She did mention a dead daughter, too."

Frost continued, his Blackwing 602 still tucked into his blonde afro. "Cecil Castellan was her last husband—the richest of them all, and the one she loved most. Adrian and Gabriel were her favourites." He leaned in slightly, lowering his voice, clearly enjoying the attention from his three companions. "You know what she did? Even before Cecil kicked the bucket, Livia changed the last names of her other sons to Castellan. Some of them hated it. But they didn't have a choice. Had to do what Mommy wanted."

Naomi shuffled closer to Clayton. "The Castellan sons are a strange lot. They hardly get along."

"That'll be one hell of a fight for her fortune if she doesn't leave an ironclad will," Frost said, biting his thick red lips as he paused.

Before he could say another word, applause and cheers erupted.

Clayton turned his head toward the grand entrance.

The Castellans had finally arrived.

THE LIVE ORCHESTRA PLAYED MELLOW MUSIC, ITS MELODIES WEAVING through the hall without overpowering the hum of conversation. Clayton stood with Frost and Johnson, watching Elijah Brooks and his wife engage with the Castellan clan.

Not far from them, Naomi stood with her usual elegance, poised yet watchful.

Clayton's gaze shifted to Livia Castellan, noting how her five sons surrounded her—not protectively, but as if each was vying for her attention.

"Pretty damn obvious," Johnson muttered. "The way they all kiss up to her."

"Sycophants," Frost said. "Her own kids, having to stoop that low. Tells you a lot about her personality, doesn't it?"

Clayton nodded.

Frost gestured toward the family with a slight tilt of his chin. "Dominic—the tall one. He's the oldest, a product of the first husband and a nasty divorce. But he's strong-willed. I've met them all." He took a breath before continuing. "The one with the shaved head and glasses? That's Matteo Castellan. Smart, strategic—the thinker of the family. And the one with the long black hair? Luca Castellan. The playboy. Got all the charm and charisma."

Johnson pivoted slightly, his gaze locking onto Livia and her sons. "And what about the timid one? The one still tied to Mommy's apron strings?"

Clayton had to grin. Johnson wasn't far off.

Frost chuckled. "That's Adrian Castellan. The quiet one. Observant. Sharp. The true Castellan. Not only will he inherit his father's fortune, but he'll likely get the lion's share of his mother's as well." Frost exhaled before adding, "Which brings us to Nico Castellan. The rebel. Fast cars, fast life, and a real problem with authority—including his mother's."

Frost's green eyes flashed with excitement. "Get this—Nico actually took his mother to court. Sued her for control of his stepfather's estate before the man even passed. Cecil Castellan wasn't his biological father, but they were close. The old man gave Nico everything he wanted—even blank checks."

Johnson shook his head. "Gotta hand it to you, Frost. How the hell do you know all this?"

Frost laughed. "I'm a reporter. It's my job to get the details."

Their conversation came to an abrupt halt as Naomi stepped away from the mayor and the Castellans, making her way toward them.

Clayton tensed.

Livia Castellan and his father were looking right at him. And Clayton knew exactly what that meant.

Naomi's expression was unreadable, but there was a flicker of concern in her eyes. She studied Clayton for a moment, as if bracing for his reaction.

"Livia Castellan wants you to meet her family," she said.

Clayton led the way.

Frost and Johnson followed.

52

Clayton stood just a step ahead of the others, facing Livia Castellan, her five sons, and his father. His gaze flicked to Mrs. Brooks, noting her beauty and the slight difference in age between her and the mayor.

Livia Castellan's gown was elegant and appropriate for her years, though nothing about it was understated. The necklace around her throat likely cost more than Clayton would earn in five years, and with every subtle movement of her hands, the gemstones on her rings caught the light.

He corrected himself before speaking, remembering how the Castellan matriarch preferred to be addressed. "Ms. Castellan." His mouth felt dry—something about this woman unsettled him. "A pleasure to meet you again. And happy birthday."

Her smile was poised but hollow. Livia extended her hand—not to be kissed, as one would a lady's, but to be shaken.

"The detective lives," she said, gripping his hand firmly. Her eyes flicked to the mayor. "Elijah mentioned your near-death experience." She turned her gaze back to Clayton, unblinking. "I hope you don't think I had anything to do with it."

Clayton's jaw tightened. A sharp flash of memory—water rushing in,

Johnson's car plunging from the bridge—cut through his mind. A smirk pulled at the corner of his lips. "Somehow, Ms. Castellan, I don't think you would have missed." He cast a glance at his father. "That shooter, whoever he was, is a lousy shot."

Johnson let out a short, involuntary laugh, but the reaction from the rest of the room was starkly different. A tension-filled silence settled over them. Clayton caught the barely audible gasp from Mrs. Brooks, the stiffness in the mayor's shoulders. Even the Castellan sons seemed momentarily stunned.

But Livia Castellan didn't flinch.

After a beat, she turned to her sons, breaking the moment. "Boys, this is Detective Muttler." Then, she looked to Johnson. "Your name again, detective?"

Johnson held her gaze, unblinking. "Johnson."

"Ah, yes. Detective Johnson." Her attention shifted beyond him to Frost. "Good to see you again, Elliot Frost."

Frost grinned. "How could I turn down an invitation, Ms. Castellan? This is quite the spectacle." He gestured lightly to the lavish hall around them.

Clayton studied the Castellan men, recalling every detail Frost had shared earlier.

Luca stepped forward first, his easy charisma apparent. "Welcome to Castellan Manor, man." He shook hands with Clayton, Johnson, and Frost in turn.

Dominic Castellan, with his mother's eyes, offered only a curt nod.

Matteo, the intellectual, adjusted his glasses with a slim finger and gave a calculating smile. "Do you think you'll catch your killer soon, detective?"

Clayton flicked his gaze toward his father, wondering just how much of the case had been shared with this family. "We're working on that."

Adrian Castellan stood closest to his mother, silent but watchful, his protective presence unmistakable. His eyes met Clayton's briefly—assessing, unreadable.

Then Nico stepped forward, bold and brash. He playfully knocked Clayton's shoulder with his fist. "Welcome to Castellan Manor—the most fucked-up place in the world."

Livia's lips pressed into a thin line, her lower lip trembling. "Nico." Her fists clenched at her sides. "It's bad enough you were late. Now mind your tongue or get out of my sight."

Without a word, Nico turned and walked out of the hall.

Luca tilted his head toward his departing brother. "Don't worry about Nico. He does this all the time." With effortless confidence, he stepped closer. "He'll be back before anyone even notices he's gone."

The scent of his cologne lingered—distinct and unforgettable, yet unfamiliar to Clayton. Luca's black hair wasn't disheveled, but it gleamed with a sheen that rivalled those Pantene commercials. There was a ruggedness to him, despite being the most impeccably dressed of the Castellan sons.

Beside him, Livia Castellan moved with silent authority, her mere presence enough to curb further conversation. With a single glance, she dismissed her sons. Three melted into the crowd without hesitation, but one remained—hovering at her side.

Adrian Castellan.

His silent plea was met with a sharp, unyielding stare. Clayton watched as his mother's jaw tightened, her expression leaving no room for disobedience. Adrian hesitated, his reluctance clear, but eventually, he turned and followed his brothers.

Clayton shifted his gaze from his father and his wife to their hostess, still piecing together the dynamics between them. His father owed Livia Castellan something—of that, Clayton was certain.

Livia turned back to him, her tone smooth but deliberate. "You'll have to forgive my sons, Mr. Muttler. When you bring someone into this world, you tend to indulge them a little too much. You love them unconditionally." Her gaze flickered—just briefly—toward Naomi before settling back on Clayton. "Maybe one day, you'll understand, detective."

A small nod. "Now, if you'll excuse me, I have other guests to attend to."

With that, Livia Castellan walked away. But Elijah Brooks remained. His eyes locked onto Clayton.

"I need to have a word with you."

Then, without waiting, Elijah Brooks turned toward the exit, expecting his son to follow.

53

His father led him just outside the mansion, near the parking area. The outdoors were well-lit, but in the distance, other structures on the estate lay in complete darkness. Clayton's eyes scanned the grounds as they stood in silence for several moments.

Elijah Brooks planted his feet apart, hands on his hips. "What the hell do you think you're doing?"

Clayton frowned. "I'm not following."

"When Naomi told me you were coming with her, I never expected you to show up with your partner and a reporter." He pointed toward the mansion. "I thought you'd come here, enjoy yourself—not stake the place out." He shook his head. "And to bring that reporter?"

"Elliot Frost had his own invitation from the Castellans," Clayton said flatly. "But let's get something straight—you don't need to expect anything of me. Like I told you before, I'm going to solve this case."

Something shifted in his father's expression—a flicker of something softer, almost vulnerable. "Look, Clayton... Clay—I don't even know what you prefer." His voice lowered. "You show up at my office, drop a bomb about being my son, then do nothing. Nothing at all. What the hell do you want from me?"

"Nothing."

Elijah exhaled a bitter laugh. "You sure about that, boy?" He didn't wait for an answer. "You've got two younger brothers and a sister. I've told them about you. You've seen my wife. Marie understands."

Clayton scoffed. "Does she know you use an anonymous site for sex? Does she understand that?"

His father's jaw tightened, but his voice remained measured. "My personal life is none of your business." He stroked his goatee, inhaling deeply. "I wasn't in your life. I never knew you existed. Your mother never told me."

Clayton's eyes burned with anger. "Don't you dare put that on her. She's dead. She's not here to defend herself." His finger jabbed the air between them.

Elijah held his ground. "Look me in the eyes and tell me you want nothing to do with me—or your siblings—and I'll leave you alone."

There was something else now. Fear.

Clayton's voice was low, sharp. "Why don't you look me in the eyes and tell me Livia Castellan has nothing over you?" He pointed again. "That's what you need to do, Mr. Mayor. Then we can talk."

That was when he felt it.

A presence.

His body tensed. In the distance, near one of the smaller structures on the grounds, a dark figure lingered. Watching. The silhouette shifted, as if realizing it had been spotted.

His father noticed Clayton's sudden stillness. "What's wrong?"

Clayton took a step forward but hesitated. "Not sure. Someone was watching us." His voice dropped as he motioned toward the mansion. "Let's go. I think our killer is here."

He stood next to Johnson at the far side of the great hall, watching the movements and interactions of Livia Castellan's guests. They had positioned themselves where they could speak privately, yet Clayton's eyes remained vigilant, scanning the room with caution. Someone at Livia Castellan's party was a murderer.

Johnson stood with both hands in his pockets. "If someone was really watching you outside, that bastard's got eyes on us now." He lowered his voice. "Did you bring your piece?"

Clayton raised a brow. "Closest thing to me right now."

Johnson nodded. "After nearly getting killed the other day, there was no way I'd come here without mine." He nudged Clayton lightly. "Well, well, well. Look who decided to join the party."

Clayton's gaze sharpened. "Mitchel Milan."

"The man of luxury," Johnson added. "Fashionably late, too."

Clayton watched the car mogul weave his way through the room. Mitchel Milan's greying hair was neatly groomed, his perfect teeth gleaming as he smiled at Livia Castellan and her sons.

"Think he was the one spying on you outside?" Johnson asked.

Clayton kept his eyes on Milan. "Can't say. But it's strange how he just showed up—less than half an hour after the mayor and I were outside talking."

"You think he heard anything? About your connection to Brooks?"

"I don't know if it was him," Clayton said, "but I saw someone in the dark. Voices carry—whoever it was could've heard us."

He scanned the crowd and let out a quiet breath when he spotted Naomi with Frost. His father and Marie had made it to the dance floor.

Nearby, Livia Castellan stood with two of her sons, Dominic and Adrian, alongside Milan. The others were nowhere to be seen.

Then Johnson nudged him again. "Look who decided to rejoin the party."

Nico Castellan entered the hall, a young woman at his side. They walked toward the dance floor, hand in hand, both disheveled. Lipstick smeared his collar and neck.

Johnson let out a low whistle.

"Save it," Clayton muttered. His voice was tight. "If our killer is here, he's watching us—right now. He has the advantage. He knows exactly who we are."

He cast a glance toward his father, still waltzing with Marie. For a moment, their eyes met. Clayton looked away—only to find Mitchel Milan watching them. A quiet exchange with Livia Castellan followed.

Something was in motion.

54

Clayton had lost sight of Naomi. Nearly an hour had passed since he'd last seen her. They'd spoken several times throughout the night, but if she wasn't by the mayor's side, she was busy with other guests.

Now, his pulse quickened as he scanned the hall.

Johnson had drifted off, now standing with Frost on the far side of the room. Clayton smirked, remembering how much his partner had initially disliked the reporter.

His father wasn't far, engaged in conversation with a group of unfamiliar faces. Livia Castellan had last been with Milan, but they, too, had disappeared into the crowd.

Clayton paced, feeling awkward—like a member of the Castellan security team rather than a guest. The thought made him chuckle, but his amusement died the moment he turned.

Naomi had just entered the hall, her steps brisk, her expression set in anger.

Then he saw why.

Nico Castellan followed, just a few strides behind her. His movements were sharp, impatient. As he reached for her arm, Clayton was already moving.

Naomi jerked away just as Clayton stepped between them. He clamped a firm hand on Nico's shoulder.

"Back off, buddy."

Nico shoved him away. "You dare talk to me like that—in my own home?"

The music stopped. Conversations died. Heads turned.

Clayton held his ground. "The lady doesn't want to be bothered."

"Clay." Naomi's voice was quiet, urgent. "Let's just go."

But Nico smirked. "She liked being bothered long before you ever came into the picture." He glanced over Clayton's shoulder. "Isn't that right, love?"

A slow burn spread through Clayton's chest. He felt Naomi tighten her grip on his arm, but before he could stop himself, he moved toward Nico—

A fist cracked against his jaw.

Nico had to hook the punch upward, but the hit landed hard. A collective gasp rippled through the hall.

Clayton barely registered the pain before his hands were on Nico's shirt, dragging him forward. Strong arms wrenched him back—two pairs, maybe more. He barely heard the voices over the rush of blood in his ears.

Then Nico's words cut through the haze.

"You think you got yourself a prize, Muttler? You think she's worth anything? I've been there!"

Clayton tore free from the hands restraining him. He swung—his fist connecting solidly. Nico staggered back, crashing to the floor.

Then—his father.

Elijah Brooks was suddenly in front of him, gripping his arms, holding him firm.

"Clay." His father's voice was low, steady. Paternal. It made him freeze.

Johnson was beside them. "Let it go, kid." His voice was calm, measured. "We've overstayed our welcome."

The group moved together—Elijah Brooks, Marie, Naomi, Frost, and Johnson. But as they stepped out of the great hall, Nico Castellan's voice carried behind them.

"You'll pay for this, Muttler!"

Outside, Elijah didn't waste a second.

"Johnson, Marie will ride with you two." He motioned to Frost. "Naomi, take Clay's car and follow me." Then, meeting Clayton's eyes, he added, "You're coming with me."

Naomi reached for Clayton's arm as he handed her the keys, but he pulled away.

55

His father's home was large, beautiful—fit for a mayor. But it was nothing compared to where he'd spent the evening. Castellan Manor had been massive.

Now, as Clayton sat in his father's study, pressing an ice pack to his jaw, he wondered what secrets this house held. What secrets his father kept. How different was Elijah Brooks from Livia Castellan?

The mayor sat behind his oak desk, watching him. They were alone—exactly how his father wanted it.

Marie had ushered the others away the moment they arrived, as if she knew her husband would want time alone with him.

For a moment, Clayton considered how everyone in his life had kept something from him. His mother—hiding his father's identity. Naomi—hiding her past with Nico Castellan. And God knew what the man staring at him now was keeping.

All the events that had unraveled since he took on this case flooded his mind. Evelyn Greene. Sabine Aldrich. And so many others. Dead.

His father's voice pulled him back.

"Naomi is a nice girl, Clay."

A jolt ran through him. Hearing his father say his name—so casually, like a father—felt strange.

"She could have mentioned she and Nico had a past," Clayton said, voice tight. "All this time—"

A slap echoed as Elijah's palm met the desk.

"Why would she be obligated to tell you that?" His father's brows pulled together. "Have you told her every detail about every girl you've been involved with?"

Clayton felt his temper rise. "Have you—"

"You will not speak about my personal business in this house."

His father leaned forward, voice firm. "This is my home. My kids are upstairs. Right now, this isn't about me. It's about you and Naomi. That girl has been like a daughter to me. I've known her for years—and I've never seen her as happy as she is with you."

Clayton exhaled sharply and let the silence settle.

Again, his father had calmed him. And as they held each other's gaze, Clayton wasn't sure what he was feeling anymore.

Elijah rose from his chair, circling the desk before stopping in front of him. "Let me see."

He reached for the ice pack. Clayton pulled away, but his father caught his wrist, firmly moving the pack from his face.

Clayton let him.

Felt vulnerable.

Like a child.

"That kid's got a good right hook." Elijah smirked. "But at least yours sent him flying."

A pause.

"Nico had it coming." His father added.

His father tilted his chin, turning his face into the light. His touch was careful, almost reverent. "You'll have this bruise for a couple of weeks."

Then, his hand drifted behind Clayton's neck, squeezing gently. Not like a doctor checking for injury. But like a father.

Clayton froze.

They locked eyes.

He couldn't speak.

Elijah knelt beside him, steadying himself on one knee. "I wouldn't dare offer you anything material." His voice was softer now. "All I have is me. You're my son, and whether you accept that or not—I need to apologize. For what I did. For what I didn't do. I'm sorry for not knowing."

The words hit like a blow.

His father's face blurred.

Clayton tried not to blink, tried to fight the sting in his eyes. But when he finally closed them, the tears came.

Elijah pulled him close. Clayton felt himself break. His body sagged, the fight leaving him as he buried his face in his father's shoulder.

A sob tore from his throat.

His father held him tighter. "It's okay. You're my son. It's okay, Clay."

He found Naomi outside, standing alone by the pool.

The night was still. The moon hung full and bright, casting silver light across the water's surface. The air was cool, and as Clayton stepped toward her, he noticed the way she held herself—arms wrapped around her body, as if shielding herself from more than just the cold.

His father's words echoed in his mind. *Say nothing of Nico Castellan.*

So he didn't.

Instead, he approached her from behind, sliding his arms gently around her waist. Naomi tensed—only for a moment—before sinking against him. He exhaled, pressing his cheek against her hair, letting his own body relax in turn.

And in that moment, he knew.

He loved her.

He didn't need to say it. Not now. He just felt it. And somehow, he knew she felt it too.

For the first time in a long time, Clayton let everything else fall away.

The case. The deaths. The attempt on his life. The years of abandonment.

None of it mattered.

Not here. Not with her.

He held Naomi tighter, anchoring himself in this one fleeting moment of peace.

Because right now, she was all that mattered.

It was late. Clayton and Naomi had spent some time out by the pool, only to discover that Johnson and Frost had left when they went back inside the house.

His father followed them to the door. "The house is big enough. You're welcome to stay." His eyes were pleading.

But Clayton pulled Naomi close to him. "We should get going," he said. "But I'd like to come back... another time."

Father and son exchanged nods.

Clayton's mind and heart were full. He could hardly believe what had transpired within his father's study, and though he felt a tinge of embarrassment, something about being close to Elijah Brooks made him feel safe.

His father placed a hand on his shoulder. "Take care of that bruise."

Right then, Clayton heard footsteps tumbling down the circular staircase.

His three siblings.

His identical twin brothers had bright, happy smiles, and his sister was as beautiful as her mother.

Their father eyed them with scrutiny, but Clayton saw pride in his eyes. Love. "I thought you three were asleep, huh?"

The first twin spoke first, his eyes fixed on Clayton. "Mom told us he was here."

Their mother descended the stairs gracefully. "I wanted you to meet your brothers and sister," she said. Marie nudged her daughter forward. "This is Sierra."

The twin who spoke first took Clayton's hand. "I'm Hugo." He pointed to his brother. "And this is my little brother, Heath."

Heath seemed less social than his brother, but he was pleasant. Polite. Instead of a handshake, he gave Clayton a hug. "I've always wanted a big brother."

Hugo playfully shoved his identical half. "And what am I, you idiot?"

Heath shoved back. "You're like three minutes older, Hugo. You don't count."

Clayton grinned as his three siblings laughed at each other. He exchanged a final look with his father and a thankful nod to Marie before leading Naomi out the door.

56

A white Bentley Flying Spur pulled into the underground parking lot. Inside, the lone passenger received final instructions: remove the VR headset, don the mask.

Within moments, his world narrowed to the slits of an elegant Anubis mask. The black box was left on the back seat—he wouldn't need it anymore.

Tonight, the jackal-headed god was in search of his perfect match. It was why he had come. His goddess was waiting.

He stepped out of the Bentley, pulse steady, anticipation coiled beneath the surface. The path led him to an elevator, the ride up smooth and silent. He didn't count the floors—there was no need.

When the doors parted, music drifted in. The lounge was exquisite, as expected. Velvet seating. Soft golden lighting. The air carried the scent of expensive perfume and subtle intrigue. Around him, others waited—alphas in their chosen masks, poised for their anonymous counterparts to arrive.

Anubis waited. He would know her when he saw her. He would know the mask.

A black wall slid apart, revealing the adjoining room. The others stood waiting. And then—he saw her.

Bastet.

Sleek, feline. The gold and black details of her mask complemented the jackal's sharp, angular form. A perfect match.

His gloved fingers steepled before him. She had seen him too. No hesitation. Only certainty.

Their strides were deliberate, measured. They met at the centre, hands grazing before fingers laced together. No words were spoken. There was no need.

A room awaited beyond the stairs.

Together, they ascended.

57

With everything they'd gathered so far, Clayton and Johnson sat at their desks, trying to piece together the case. Clayton's jaw throbbed with every turn of his head, every slight movement. Even speaking made him wince.

"So, we know our latest victim, Lexx, was killed by the same guy," Clayton said, sliding Lexx's photo beneath those of Evelyn Greene and Sabine Aldrich. "CODIS confirmed it."

Johnson nodded, rubbing his chin. "And we've got his practice kills. But I'm telling you, kid—I think Milan's our guy." He tapped Mitchel Milan's name on their growing list. "He's got access to all the clients. His cars picked up Evelyn and Sabine." Johnson leaned back, eyes narrowing. "Who else could've been watching you and your old man outside the Castellan mansion?"

Clayton stiffened. His father. The memory of their embrace flashed through his mind, catching him off guard. He hadn't spoken to him since that night. His jaw tightened—wrong move. A fresh bolt of pain shot through him.

"Anyone," he muttered. "Anyone could've been watching."

Johnson studied him for a moment. "So, you're thinking Nico?"

Clayton exhaled sharply. "I don't know what to think." But Nico's words still echoed in his head. *You think you got yourself a prize, Muttler? I've been there...*

Johnson must've picked up on it. His voice softened. "Hey, kid... don't let anyone or anything come between you and the one you love." He paused, as if speaking from experience. "Naomi's a great girl. Just saying."

Clayton gave a stiff nod. The night of the party, he and Naomi had been inseparable. But since Monday morning, nothing. It was now Tuesday. He shook off the thought, forcing himself to focus. "Why Stonebrook?"

Johnson frowned. "Not following."

"Why so many girls from there? Could the killer be from Stonebrook?" Clayton rubbed his bruised jaw absently.

"It's a small town," Johnson said. "Mostly working class."

"No, we're missing something."

Johnson let out a slow exhale. "You think there's a connection between Stonebrook and the killings here?"

Clayton nodded. His gut told him there was something bigger at play.

Johnson sighed. "Maybe you're right. But I smell Anonyme written all over this. Livia Castellan and our boy Milan? They're in this deep."

58

Bastet's eyes fluttered open to complete darkness. A wave of dizziness washed over her. Her body felt sluggish, weak. She shifted, only to realize her hands were bound behind her back. Panic surged through her veins. She wriggled, testing the restraints.

She didn't know where she was.

The mask was still affixed to her face—she could feel its elegant contours against her skin—but she saw nothing. Something covered her head. A bag. A sheet. Something.

The feline goddess felt helpless. A shiver coursed through her spine as awareness settled in—she was being watched.

Someone was there.

Her breath hitched. Anubis. The jackal god. His black mask was the last thing she remembered. Then, piece by piece, the night started to come back.

The lavish room beyond the stairs

The champagne

The caviar

The bed.

Her pulse pounded in her skull.

Then—movement. A shuffle of feet. The creak of wood under careful steps.

Her wrists ached against the restraints. She swallowed, forcing air into her lungs.

"Who's there?" she whispered, her voice unsteady.

No answer.

Long, deep breaths. She had to think. Had to stay calm.

What had she gotten herself into?

HE WATCHED HER.

She lay on the floor just feet away, motionless except for the slow rise and fall of her breath. Bastet—the goddess who thought herself clever. Bastet, who believed she could move unseen.

But she had sought him out. And now, she would die.

Not yet, though. Not before he was ready. She would be his masterpiece, the one they would all remember. A vision of divinity, laid bare for the world to see. This time, there would be no deception.

His jaw clenched at the memory of the last one—the one who betrayed him. The one who wasn't a woman.

His fingers curled into fists, rage simmering in his chest. He had been fooled, humiliated. That mistake would not happen again. Bastet would put things back in order. She would restore the balance. She would be his redemption.

His eyes flicked over her, the temptation to act now almost unbearable. But patience was key. Precision. The ritual had to be perfect.

On the floor, she stirred. A slow inhale. Then—

"What do you want from me?" Her voice was unsteady, raw with fear. "Who... who are you?"

He didn't answer. Not yet.

Soon, she would see him. Soon, she would understand.

59

Elliot Frost stormed into the mayor's office, his heart sinking as he spotted Naomi's empty desk. He didn't need to look any further; she hadn't shown up for work that morning.

The other assistant, pleasant and unsuspecting, greeted him, but Elliot didn't slow down. He bypassed her desk with purpose. He needed to speak with the mayor—and fast.

"Excuse me, Sir. You can't go in there."

But Elliot was already past her, pushing through the door.

Mayor Brooks spun around abruptly from the window, his eyes burning with surprise and irritation.

Before Brooks could utter a word, Elliot's words tumbled out, unrestrained, the weight of urgency finally breaking through. Naomi had sworn him to secrecy, but it didn't matter now. "Mayor Brooks, has Naomi shown up for work this morning?"

Brooks froze, brow furrowing in confusion. "What's this all about?"

Elliot's voice dropped, serious. "Sir, I think Naomi's in danger... and Clayton knows nothing about it."

THE MOMENT CLAYTON SAW ELLIOT FROST AND HIS FATHER APPROACH HIS desk, he knew something was wrong. He and Johnson were on their feet before they even reached them.

"Naomi didn't show up for work today," his father said.

Clayton's stomach twisted. He looked at Johnson, already seeing the same thought forming in his partner's mind.

Frost pressed his lips together, hesitation flickering across his face before he admitted, "Naomi... she told me you knew what she was doing."

Clayton's pulse spiked. He stepped toward the reporter, his voice sharp. "What are you talking about?"

"The night of the party," Frost exhaled, running a hand through his silver-white hair. "She came up with a plan—to go to Anonyme. As a client."

Johnson swore under his breath. "What the fuck." He didn't seem to care that the mayor was standing right there.

Clayton barely heard him. A sickening weight pressed against his chest. He turned to his father, whose expression remained unreadable. "When was the last time you saw Naomi?"

Clayton opened his mouth, but his brain stalled. The truth was, he hadn't seen her since—

"Clay!" His father's voice cut through the fog.

Clayton shook his head, grounding himself. "Yesterday. In the morning."

Johnson shifted his weight. "Alright, Frost. Start talking. What the hell happened?"

Frost sighed. "She said she wanted to help. That you," he looked at Clayton, guilt thick in his voice, "gave her the go-ahead."

Clayton barely resisted the urge to punch something. "I never—" He exhaled sharply. "What was her plan?"

Frost hesitated, then spoke quickly, as if he needed to get it out. "We both created accounts. We picked masks so we'd know each other right away." He stopped, rubbing a hand down his face. "I was supposed to be

Anubis. She was Bastet. I was at the place, but Naomi never showed up. No one had on a Bastet mask."

A cold sweat broke across Clayton's back.

Johnson frowned. "Then where did her ride take her?"

Clayton turned away, his fists clenched. She was out there. Somewhere. In a stranger's car, driving to God knows where.

Johnson glared at Frost. "What the fuck did you two think you were going to find?"

Frost exhaled, avoiding Clayton's gaze.

Clayton already knew the answer. He ran a hand down his face. "She wanted to use herself as bait."

The words tasted like acid.

Frost nodded stiffly.

Clayton's hands curled into fists. His gut told him her decision had everything to do with that night at Livia Castellan's mansion. The confrontation with Nico Castellan.

Frost swallowed, his emerald eyes downcast.

Clayton turned to his father, voice tight. "Anonyme. Livia Castellan. Everything points to that family. Now Naomi is gone."

His father exhaled. "Clay, I've known the woman for years. Do you really think she's capable of killing young girls?"

"She may not be the killer," Clayton said, "but I think she knows who is."

Johnson crossed his arms. "Or she's protecting him."

Brooks shook his head, rubbing his jaw. "Come on. You really think Livia Castellan is capable of this? She may look like a billion dollars, but she isn't young."

Johnson scoffed. "Doesn't mean she's innocent."

Frost suddenly tensed. "There's something else. I tried logging into my account this morning." He glanced up at Clayton. "It was gone. Deleted."

A beat of silence passed.

Johnson snapped his fingers. "Quit stalling, kid. This guy has Naomi, and he's hours ahead of us."

Clayton nodded, his mind a storm of panic and fury. His pulse thundered in his ears. Naomi is out there. Naomi is out there.

He took a sharp breath. "We need to arrest Nico Castellan."

His father's voice was firm. "No."

Clayton turned on him, eyes blazing.

Brooks raised a hand before he could speak. "Livia Castellan is a clever woman. If you mess with her, you have to go prepared." His jaw tightened. "Trust me on this. If you want to arrest that kid, you'll need a damn good reason."

Clayton's breath was shallow. His muscles coiled with frustration. "What do you expect me to do? Naomi is out there."

His father didn't hesitate. He stepped forward and gripped the back of Clayton's neck—steady, grounding. "I understand, Clay," he said quietly. "But you gotta use your head. Especially when dealing with Livia Castellan."

Clayton forced himself to breathe. *Focus.*

He exhaled. "Okay. I'll… I'll talk to Dawson."

Brooks shook his head. "I'll handle Dawson later." He turned to Johnson. "You and Frost—go to Naomi's place. See what you can find."

Clayton barely nodded, his thoughts spinning like a siren. *Naomi is out there. Naomi is out there.*

Then, clarity. He looked at Johnson. "Keep me in the loop."

He turned to his father. His voice was steady, controlled. "We need to talk to Mitchel Milan." His stomach hardened with certainty. "Somehow, I think he's at the centre of all this."

His father held his gaze for a moment. Then, finally, he nodded.

"Let's go."

60

Clayton wasn't sure what he expected to find at Westbridge Executive Transport, but something was pulling him toward Kingsley Docks. One of Mitchel Milan's cars took Naomi. That was all that mattered.

With his father in the passenger seat of his Range Rover, Clayton's foot pressed hard on the accelerator. They were running out of time.

After a long, tense silence, his father finally spoke. "You think Milan has her stashed somewhere?"

Clayton gripped the wheel hard. Dark thoughts crept in, clawing at his mind. *What if Naomi was already dead? What if he was too late?* His stomach twisted. He slapped the wheel, forcing the thought away. "I don't know."

He eased off the gas as the bridge came into view.

The bridge where he and Johnson were nearly killed.

His hands went clammy. His eyes flicked to the temporary repairs—the spot where Johnson's car had gone off the edge. The trauma hit him like a fist to the chest. It was as if the world was closing in around him.

"Clay." His father's voice cut through the spiral, grounding him. A firm hand on his shoulder. "Settle yourself."

Clayton exhaled sharply and gave a quick nod, focusing back on the road. "Milan—his cars—one of them picked her up." The words came quicker now, urgency taking over. "The day of the crash, Johnson and I were heading to Milan's place. We never made it there."

"You think he knew you were coming?"

"Someone did." Clayton's jaw tightened. "We headed for the docks after Orbis Noir. We'd just gotten the Anonyme list."

A pause.

Clayton glanced at his father, recalling something from that list. A detail that had seemed insignificant at the time.

His father must have noticed his expression. "What is it?"

Clayton shook his head, thinking out loud. "Mitchel Milan's name wasn't on the list."

His father frowned. "And?"

"It doesn't add up." Clayton's mind was racing now. "Someone like Milan—who has access to all these high-end clients—should be using the service."

"Maybe she struck his name off," his father said.

"Or maybe Milan has more at stake in Anonyme than we thought." The idea settled uneasily in Clayton's gut. Livia Castellan wasn't just protecting clients. She was hiding something.

The glass warehouse of Westbridge Executive Transport loomed ahead. Peaceful. Still.

But Clayton was ready to tear the place apart to get Naomi back.

He set his jaw, gripping the wheel tighter. "Follow my lead when we get there."

His father nodded.

Elliot Frost's call came through just as Clayton put the Range Rover into park. As he accepted, he could hear Johnson's voice in the background.

"Anything at Naomi's place?" Clayton exhaled, letting his head drop back against the headrest.

Frost's voice still carried the weight of guilt. "Nothing. But Johnson and I found something else." A beat. Then urgency crept into his tone. "We're at the library, digging through old census records."

Johnson's gruff voice cut in. "Get this, kid—Livia Castellan and Mitchel Milan are first cousins."

Clayton turned sharply to his father. Their eyes met, both of them absorbing the revelation.

Mitchel Milan was in deep. Too deep.

Clayton's grip tightened on the door handle. He was ready to move. But Frost's voice made him pause.

"And there's more," the reporter continued. "Livia Castellan? She's a Stonebrook native. Born and raised."

A second of silence, then Johnson let out a short laugh. "And she was dirt poor."

It didn't seem real. Livia had always projected an image of wealth and exclusivity—an untouchable figure in elite circles. But suddenly, it all made sense.

Clayton glared at the warehouse. Milan knew something. He could feel it.

His father's voice, deep and thoughtful, pulled him back. "Livia's always claimed she was from way out west—never mentioned Stonebrook at all."

Clayton had heard enough. Pieces were snapping into place, but Naomi was still missing.

"Johnson, get back to the precinct. I need a warrant for Castellan Manor."

"What about Milan?"

Clayton swung open his door, jaw set.

"One way or another, he's gonna tell me where Naomi is."

Mitchel Milan's office was at the rear of the building, offering a sweeping panoramic view of the Westbridge River. But as Clayton and Elijah Brooks stepped inside, all he could see was the bridge in the distance.

The bridge where Johnson's car had plunged into the water.

Clayton's jaw tightened. Had Milan been standing here that day, watching? Or had he been the one pulling the trigger?

Milan was behind his desk, his usual polished confidence slipping the moment his eyes landed on them. He hadn't expected this. Not Clayton. And definitely not the mayor.

His gaze darted from one to the other. "Mayor Brooks." His voice was smooth, but his stance betrayed him. The man looked small in his own kingdom.

Clayton didn't waste time. He stepped forward, voice edged with fury. "I know what you and your cousin have been hiding."

A quick glance from his father.

Milan's expression barely flickered, but his eyes—they gave him away. He knew exactly what Clayton was talking about.

Still, he opened his mouth to deny it.

Clayton didn't let him. "Livia Castellan's son took Naomi." His voice was a growl. "I know it. Where is she?"

Beside him, Brooks caught the rhythm and pressed in. "Make no mistake, Mitchel—I'll use every power at my disposal to tear down everything you've built." He took a slow step toward the desk. "Tell my son where the girl is."

For a moment, Milan said nothing. Then, the smallest flicker of a smile touched the corner of his mouth.

"So it's true," he murmured. His gaze flicked between them, settling on Brooks. "The detective is your son."

Clayton studied his father's face, looking for a reaction.

Brooks only shrugged. "Old news." His voice was casual. Dismissive. "But that's the least of your problems."

Clayton took his cue. "Mitchel Milan, you're under arrest. For your role in the murders."

Milan staggered back, crashing into his chair. His hands flew up, palms out. "Look, I had nothing to do with those killings." His voice was higher now, shaking. "My cousin—Livia and I—we're business partners. I handle the rides for the service, that's it—"

Clayton was over him in an instant, hands pressed hard against the desk. "Then how the hell did you know Naomi was supposed to meet Frost last night? Why didn't she show up?"

Milan stammered. "I—I don't know! Like I said, I don't have access to client accounts. My job is logistics. Pickups. Drop-offs."

Clayton's hands fisted in Milan's collar before he could stop himself. The man flinched, eyes wide with fear.

Behind him, his father's firm grip landed on his shoulder, grounding him.

Brooks didn't pull him back—he let him press the fear deeper into Milan. But his focus remained steady. "One of your cars picked up Naomi. Another picked up Frost. He arrived at the venue." His voice darkened. "She didn't."

Milan swallowed hard, yanking a tablet from his desk. His fingers shook as he swiped through screens. Then, his face paled.

"There were two venues," he mumbled. "Monday was a busy night."

Clayton's heart pounded. "The names. Look them up."

Milan's hand raked through his disheveled hair. "It doesn't work like that. No names. Just the masks."

Clayton's breath caught. The masks.

His eyes snapped shut as realization hit. "Anubis... and Bastet."

Slowly, Milan glanced up. "They were taken to separate locations."

Clayton turned to his father, stomach dropping. "Frost said they were supposed to be at the same venue."

It wasn't just a mix-up. Someone diverted Naomi.

His father exhaled. His voice dropped to something quieter, heavier. "You're going to prison, Mitchel. That much is certain. The only thing you get to decide is how long you'll be in there."

Milan's gaze flickered toward the mayor, then back to Clayton.

"Livia isn't the type of person you cross," he said, voice barely above a whisper. "Even you should know that."

Clayton leaned in, his voice steel. "If her son does anything to Naomi, you'll be wishing you had her to deal with." He unhooked the cuffs from his belt.

"Mitchel Milan, you're under arrest."

61

The Range Rover tore down the narrow road toward Castellan Manor, every bump and sharp turn rattling Johnson in the passenger seat. He braced himself, gripping the handle above the door.

"You still think we've got the element of surprise?" His voice shook as they hit another dip. "If Castellan knew we were coming to her office the first time, someone's given her a heads-up about the warrant."

Clayton kept his eyes on the road. "At least we know it won't be Mitchel Milan. I told the boys to keep him on ice for a few hours. No phone calls."

Johnson scoffed. "Doesn't mean Livia doesn't have eyes in the precinct. Or the judge's office. Kid, you'd be shocked at what money buys these days."

"If that's the case, she's probably made sure Nico Castellan's out of the country."

Johnson turned his head. "So you're sure he's our guy?" There was doubt in his voice.

Clayton hesitated. "Milan didn't deny it when I said we'd be heading to the mansion."

"He didn't confirm it either." Johnson studied him. "The woman's got five sons. What exactly did you say to Milan?"

Clayton ran it back in his head. His jaw tightened. Holy shit.

Johnson sat up. "What?"

"I told him we knew what he and Livia were hiding... I mentioned the warrant... but I never said a name."

Realization hit like a brick. He'd assumed Nico—because of their history, because of that punch to the face. But was he chasing the right ghost?

Johnson exhaled hard. "Slow down for a second, kid."

Clayton shot him a glare. "What?"

"Let's think this through."

"We don't have time." Clayton slammed on the brakes, dust kicking up around them. "Naomi's out there. Every second counts."

Johnson held up his hands. "And I'm telling you—you've got blinders on. You're zeroed in on Nico Castellan because of your history with him. Because he's got ties to Naomi. But take a step back. What if we're looking at the wrong brother?"

Clayton's grip tightened on the wheel. He hated it—hated that Johnson had a point.

Johnson popped open the door, stepped out, ran a hand through his hair. He took a deep breath before climbing back in.

"Livia knows who the killer is," he said. "Guarantee it. And if Nico was involved, she wouldn't let him anywhere near the mansion. Naomi's not there."

Clayton swore under his breath. He'd wasted time.

"What now?"

Johnson tapped the dashboard. "Think about what Frost told us. Livia Castellan is from Stonebrook."

Clayton nodded. "You think she's got property there?"

"She's sentimental. Someone like her—grows up dirt poor, builds an empire—she holds onto something from where she came from." Johnson turned to him. "I'll bet my pension she still owns something out there."

Clayton reached for the ignition, but Johnson stopped him with a firm grip on his arm.

"Call Frost," Johnson said. "Now. We need to know if Castellan's got ties to Stonebrook—fast."

THEY WERE ALREADY ON THEIR WAY WHEN FROST CALLED BACK WITH THE information they needed. Johnson's hunch had paid off. Livia Castellan still owned property in her old town.

Clayton's foot pressed down hard on the accelerator. 237 Holden Street, Stonebrook was fifteen minutes away. Naomi's life depended on every second.

"Easy, kid," Johnson said, trying to sound relaxed, though his grip on the door told a different story. "We wanna get there in one piece."

Clayton barely heard him. Every second lost meant Naomi was in more danger. He had to tell himself she was still alive. There was no other option. Flashes of himself standing over his mother's open grave a year before haunted him. He couldn't go through that again. Not with Naomi.

He drove in silence, his thoughts racing, until something clicked. "Someone with access to Anonyme's system deleted Elliot's profile," Clayton said. "And that same person made sure he and Naomi never found each other."

Johnson exhaled. "Anubis and Bastet." He braced himself as Clayton took another sharp turn. "I know where you're going with this, kid. You think one of the sons—Nico Castellan specifically—has access to Anonyme's database?"

"I think Livia Castellan knows one of her sons is a killer," Clayton said. His eyes flicked to the GPS screen. "And I believe Milan when he said he only arranges the rides for clients. But someone else has access to everything—billing details, full names, addresses."

Johnson scrolled through the photos Frost had sent. His brow furrowed. "Castellan's old house is in the roughest part of town. Life must've been tough for her."

Clayton shot him a glance. "Feeling sorry for her?"

"Not a chance, kid."

They drove in tense silence until Clayton veered off the main road. They were close.

Holden Street was exactly what he'd pictured—weathered houses, abandoned lots, rundown gas stations, liquor stores. It had the kind of rough, working-class feel that people like Livia Castellan spent their whole lives trying to erase.

Clayton removed his weapon from its holster. "We go in on foot from here."

Johnson nodded, already pulling out his gun.

They were about to step out when Clayton's phone rang.

His father.

THERE WAS URGENCY IN HIS FATHER'S VOICE AS IT BLARED ON SPEAKERPHONE. Clayton and Johnson sat inside the Range Rover, both holding their weapons in hand.

"Something isn't right." His father said. "Livia Castellan just left my office, Clay. With her five sons."

Clayton looked to Johnson, mouth ajar. The words didn't register at first. His entire focus had been on this house—this moment. But if all five sons were with Livia, then who the hell was inside?

Johnson broke the silence. "If we're here outside her old house and she's all the way there with the boys, who the hell's got Naomi?"

Clayton's mind was racing. Did they drive nearly an hour to a dead end? His grip tightened on his gun as his pulse hammered in his ears. His gut had never steered him wrong before. Every instinct told him Naomi was here. But now, doubt clawed at the edges of his certainty.

Finally, he found words, shaking off the shock. "Milan is still in lockup."

"Then who's been killing those girls if not one of Livia Castellan's sons?" Johnson's gaze was fixed on the house several doors down.

A memory flickered in Clayton's mind—something that had been bothering him since this all started. The victims. All of them connected to Anonyme. Someone with access had been erasing records, rerouting rides. Milan was a middleman. The sons were accounted for. But Livia—Livia had been protecting someone.

His father's voice crackled over the speaker again, lower this time. "Clay... be careful."

There was something else there, something his father wasn't saying.

A hesitation.

A weight in his voice.

Not about the case. About him.

Clayton's throat tightened. He wasn't sure why, but he suddenly felt like a kid again, standing in some doorway, waiting for a father who never came.

Brooks exhaled. "I mean it." His voice was steady, but the edges of it—Clayton caught them this time. A crack beneath the mayor's usual polish. Worry.

Maybe something more.

Clayton opened his mouth, but Johnson spoke first. "Then they've hired someone to keep her here."

Clayton exhaled sharply, gripping the door handle. "We're going in."

Another pause.

His father's voice was quiet now, like something he wasn't sure how to say was stuck in his throat. "Clay—"

Clayton stopped, waiting.

Brooks hesitated, then sighed. "...Just don't do anything reckless." It wasn't what he wanted to say. They both knew it.

Clayton swallowed, forcing a smirk. "You sound like a dad."

A beat of silence.

Then his father said, "Maybe I am."

The words hit harder than Clayton expected. He looked away, jaw clenching.

Johnson, being Johnson, let out a dry chuckle. "Don't worry, Mister Mayor. I'll be alright."

Clayton shook off the moment, forcing himself back into the present. "Johnson, you're an ass."

"Alright, kid, let's go."

62

His tools were laid out. Every item had its place. He'd removed her dress, leaving her in nothing but her undergarments. But those would soon be stripped away. Naomi Ellis had done everything he'd asked. She would be his next masterpiece. And Clayton Muttler would never forget him.

She was still Bastet. The mask and black velvet sack covered her head, shielding her from the truth. But now, it was time. Time she saw his face. Time for her to die.

Then, his work would begin. He'd already chosen where she would be laid after she was reborn.

Civic Tower.

He stood just feet away, watching her. She knew he was there. His lair was warm, yet she trembled. He could hear her sharp, uneven breaths beneath the black sack. Bastet, the goddess, was afraid.

He leaned in slightly. "N-no one will h-hear you if y-you scream," he murmured. "N-not a soul."

The sudden intake of her breath pleased him. He stepped closer, floorboards creaking beneath his weight. Her hands hugged her body, as if she could make herself smaller, disappear.

Slowly, carefully, he loosened the sack. But as always, the moment came—the wave of shame crashing over him, the sting of insecurity burrowing deep. He hated this part. Hated the way they always looked at him.

He pulled the sack away.

For a moment, all he saw was the golden-black elegance of Bastet. But then, beyond the slanted slits of the mask, he saw her eyes.

Recognition flickered. Then confusion.

She gasped, pressing back against the wall.

Her voice came as a whisper. "You... how?"

His chest tightened. The moment—the one he both feared and craved—was here.

Then, the alarm shattered it.

A shrill, piercing sound. Someone was inside the house.

Upstairs.

CLAYTON HAD DECIDED AGAINST ANNOUNCING THEIR PRESENCE AT 237 Holden Street. He stood back, watching as Johnson worked the lock with practiced precision. The door clicked open. They slipped inside.

And froze.

From the outside, Castellan's old house was a ruin—weathered, neglected, the yard overgrown. But inside? The contrast stole Clayton's breath.

The space was pristine. The original floorboards had been stained a deep, rich brown, gleaming under soft lighting. Though sparsely furnished, every fixture was elegant. Purposeful. Controlled.

Johnson eased the door shut behind them. Ahead, a staircase stretched upward. To the right, another door—locked. The basement.

Clayton caught Johnson's signal—he was heading up. Clayton nodded, moving toward the basement door. He tried the handle. Locked.

His gut twisted. Naomi was here. He felt it, an instinct he couldn't explain.

Johnson reappeared moments later, descending the stairs with a curt shake of his head. Clear.

Silent, precise, they checked the rest of the main floor. Nothing.

Their gazes met. The basement.

Clayton exhaled, his father's words echoing in his mind: *Don't do anything reckless.* But how could he have been wrong? He knew Castellan was protecting someone. They'd missed something. Someone.

A tap to his shoulder pulled him back. Focus. Whoever had shot at them on that bridge was here. They had to be ready.

Clayton stepped aside, giving Johnson the go-ahead to breach the door—

A voice crackled through the house.

Both men jerked, weapons raised, eyes darting. Where?

Then Clayton saw them. The speakers mounted along the walls.

The voice came again, warped and stuttering.

"T-touch th-that door, D-detective... and t-the girl d-dies..."

Clayton's pulse slammed against his ribs.

They were being watched.

And he knew they were here.

Clayton needed to make a decision—fast. But he hesitated, his father's warning still echoing. *Don't do anything reckless.*

But Naomi was here. Right beneath his feet.

Johnson's voice was low, urgent. "Kid, this guy's got eyes on us. What's the play?"

Clayton didn't move. *Think.* He shut his eyes for a split second, replaying what he'd seen on their approach.

The garage.

This guy was too careful—he wouldn't have just one way out. If they waited, they'd lose him.

Clayton's eyes snapped open. "Move. Now."

He took off toward the front door, Johnson on his heels.

"What's going on, kid?"

Clayton's breath came hard. "The bastard's running."

They barely hit the front steps when the garage door exploded outward—wood splintering, metal shrieking. An old Ford Maverick tore through it, tires screaming.

Clayton acted on instinct. He holstered his gun—reckless, maybe, but he didn't think. He moved.

Launching himself from the steps, he landed hard on the hood of the truck. Pain shot up his arms, but he gritted his teeth. *Hold on.*

JOHNSON BARELY CAUGHT A GLIMPSE OF THE DRIVER. BUT IN THE PASSENGER seat—Naomi.

She was masked. Bastet.

He bolted for the Range Rover, eyes locked on the old truck. On Clayton.

"Son of a bitch," he panted. "I'm getting too damn old for this."

By the time he reached the driver's side, the truck was almost at the end of the block.

His fingers fumbled with the door handle, pulse hammering. He squinted at the fleeing vehicle—just for a second, the driver's face came into view.

Something about it nagged at him. Familiar. A flicker of recognition, just out of reach. *I've seen that face before. But where?*

"Clay—holy shit!" Johnson barked.

Clayton was holding onto the hood of the truck. Holding on for his life.

Johnson shoved the thought aside, dropped into the driver's seat, and threw the Range Rover into gear.

The chase was on.

63

Clayton clung to the hood of the truck, fingers burning, nails scraping metal. The engine roared beneath him, the wind screaming past his ears. The truck was going too fast—too reckless, too desperate. His muscles screamed, but he held on, teeth clenched, because Naomi was inside.

She was curled in the passenger seat, masked—Bastet. But it wasn't just fear in her wide, frantic eyes. It was something deeper. Shame. Humiliation. Rage coiled in Clayton's chest, sharp and searing. The bastard had stripped her down.

His grip tightened. He wouldn't let go. He couldn't. Naomi's life depended on it.

And then, he had to look.

Had to see the man behind the wheel.

His gaze snapped to the driver, and for a moment, all he saw was movement—the sharp angles of a face in motion, eyes flicking between the road and the rearview. The driver yanked the wheel hard, trying to shake him off. Clayton's body slammed against the hood, pain knifing through his ribs.

He didn't let go.

And then, the driver glanced at him.

A second. Just a second.

But that was all it took.

The world seemed to shrink, sound collapsing in on itself.

Those eyes—Clayton knew those eyes.

A scar slashed down the right side of his face, twisting his lip into something almost inhuman. But it was his gaze—cold, hollow, burning with fury—that struck Clayton like a fist to the gut.

No.

No, it couldn't be.

But it was.

He wasn't staring into the eyes of just any killer.

He was staring into the eyes of a Castellan.

The resemblance was uncanny. An exact replica of Adrian Castellan. The quiet one. The obedient one. The son who never strayed from his mother's side.

Clayton's stomach turned. His fingers nearly slipped.

Because this wasn't Adrian.

Six sons. Not five.

Livia Castellan's secret had just been exposed.

Gabriel Castellan was alive.

And he was the monster they'd been hunting all along.

64

Clayton's fingers burned, raw and slick with blood. The hood of the truck was hot against his body, the wind ripping at him as the vehicle hurtled forward. His grip was failing.

Gabriel Castellan's hands were tight on the wheel, his jaw clenched, eyes alight with something dark and ruthless. Determination. Intent. Murder.

Clayton's arms screamed from the strain. His muscles felt like they would tear. He was seconds away from being thrown off.

And all he could think about—all that filled his mind—was loss.

Naomi.

He couldn't lose her.

He had already lost too much. His mother, gone. His father—still a stranger. He had barely even begun to know the man, and now, he was about to lose him too.

And Johnson.

Where was Johnson? Was he even still in the chase? There was no time to look back. No time to do anything but hold on.

And then he locked eyes with Gabriel.

Cold, scarred, filled with fury.

Clayton's breath hitched. He was staring into the eyes of a man who wanted him dead.

Gabriel jerked the wheel again, trying to shake him off, but Clayton refused to let go. He had to keep steady—impossible as it was. Had to keep those deadened, evil eyes locked on him.

Anything to make Gabriel forget about Naomi.

But then—Naomi changed everything.

Bound hands. Masked face. She was still Bastet.

And then—she moved.

Her body twisted sharply in the seat. Fast. Unnaturally fast. Too fast.

Clayton's eyes widened. Bare feet. A perfect arc. A flash of movement.

The impact was brutal. Naomi's heel cracked against Gabriel's face.

Gabriel grunted, head snapping to the side. The truck wobbled. Slowed. The wild swerving stopped.

Clayton felt the shift instantly. This was it.

Gabriel would turn his rage on Naomi now.

Clayton had to move. Had to act.

Now.

GABRIEL CASTELLAN WAS DISTRACTED. NAOMI'S BRAVERY HAD BOUGHT Clayton seconds—seconds he couldn't waste.

He locked eyes with the scarred monster, watching Gabriel snarl as he shielded himself from Naomi's kicks, one hand gripping the wheel, knuckles white. For a brief, absurd moment, Clayton thought of Livia Castellan. Why had she buried this son from the world? Why had she let everyone believe he was dead?

Then Clayton saw it. Something in Gabriel's eyes. A familiar wound. Abandonment. Isolation. The same pain that had once hollowed him out, the same rage he had felt every time his mother dodged questions about his father.

But no. Gabriel didn't deserve his empathy.

Clayton gritted his teeth and shoved the past down. The truck was slowing. Naomi had made a difference. He crawled forward, dragging his battered body across the hood, his torn fingers slipping against hot metal.

He knew what was coming next.

Gabriel slammed on the brakes. Hard.

Clayton's body lurched—his legs flew up as gravity tried to rip him away. But he held on, boots slamming against the windshield. The world spun. A distant screech of tires. A chorus of gasps from onlookers.

His muscles screamed, but he moved. He lunged for the driver's side, swung the door open—

Gabriel's face twisted in rage. And then the bastard was on him.

A wall of muscle slammed into him, knocking him backwards. The pavement hit like a sledgehammer. His ribs rattled. A sharp, burning pain in his back. Blood in his mouth.

The first punch snapped his head to the side. A brutal, skull-rattling hit—right where Nico had clocked him.

Clayton barely had time to spit blood before Gabriel drove another fist into his ribs. Something cracked. A sharp, jagged pain. His vision blurred.

The gun—his gun.

Gabriel had it.

Clayton's breath caught as he stared down the barrel of his own weapon.

Gabriel's face was wild, unhinged, pure fury as he pulled the trigger.

The shot exploded.

Agony. White-hot, ripping agony. His shoulder. Burning. Nerve-searing.

A second shot—louder. Closer.

Then, a body crashed down on top of him.

Johnson stood over the bodies, gun still raised, finger still on the trigger. The weight of what just happened settled in his chest.

The body on top of Clayton wasn't moving.

Johnson took a slow, measured step forward, circling them. He nudged Clayton's gun out of reach with his boot before exhaling through his nose. He'd done this before. Too many times. But taking a life—even one as rotten as Gabriel Castellan's—always took something from him in return.

He looked at the scarred face, confirming what he'd glimpsed as the truck tore away from 237 Holden Street.

"Hey, kid. You breathing?"

Clayton didn't answer right away. His chest rose and fell, gaze fixed on the sky. Then, a long exhale.

"Get him off me."

Johnson huffed. "Never disrupt a crime scene, kid. Didn't they teach you that in—"

A grunt. "Johnson, you're an ass. Now get this bastard off me."

Johnson smirked but bent down, gripping the dead weight of Gabriel's body. He hesitated for just a second, eyes locking onto that face again. That face.

"Son of a bitch." He muttered. "If it wasn't for that ugly scar, I'd swear I was looking at Livia's little pet."

"Adrian Castellan." Clayton's voice was raw. "Gabriel was alive all along."

Johnson dragged the body off him, rolling the corpse onto the pavement. He exhaled. "Clean shot." His stomach twisted. "So that's it. Castellan's dead son isn't dead after all."

But Clayton wasn't listening. He was already pushing himself up, swaying on his feet.

"Naomi."

He spun toward the truck. Empty.

Then—her voice.

"Clay!"

Clayton's head snapped toward the Range Rover.

Johnson clapped a hand on his shoulder before he could bolt. "Relax, kid. She got out before he shot you." He smirked. "Helluva woman."

Clayton didn't wait. He limped toward her, and the second Naomi was in his arms, she was holding onto him just as tightly.

Johnson chuckled, shaking his head. Tough guy or not, he liked a good ending.

Then his eyes slid back to the corpse sprawled on the pavement.

In the distance, sirens howled. Stonebrook's finest were finally on their way.

Johnson sighed. "Better late than never, I guess."

But one thing was certain.

Livia Castellan had a lot of explaining to do.

65

Livia Castellan sat behind her desk, her stare cold and unwavering. She didn't rise when Clayton and Johnson entered her office.

Clayton adjusted his arm in the sling with a wince. He hated wearing the damn thing, but he'd agreed—to keep Naomi from worrying. The bullet hadn't passed through clean, and the sling was supposed to help. Still, he resented how it restrained him, how it made him feel weak.

The businesswoman sat composed, her posture regal, with three attorneys positioned like sentinels at a separate desk just feet away.

Clayton exchanged a glance with Johnson. She'd been expecting them. And she was prepared.

What struck him wasn't the legal defence—it was her face. Livia Castellan had just lost a son. Yet she looked nothing like a grieving mother. No sorrow. No rage. No pain.

He thought of his own mother. Of what her face would have looked like if she had lost him.

As if reading his mind, Livia finally spoke.

"I must congratulate you, Detective Muttler."

She hadn't invited them to sit. A subtle power play.

Johnson cut straight through the pretence. "We'd offer our condolences, Ms. Castellan, but your son was a murderer." He jabbed a finger at her. "And you knew. You could've stopped him. Those girls would still be alive if he didn't have full access to your systems. You gave him an entire client list to choose from."

Livia didn't flinch. She only tilted her head slightly, considering them like they were an inconvenience. Then—her voice, calm, smooth:

"Which one of you shot my boy?"

Clayton lowered himself into the wingback chair across from her, ignoring her power play. "I think you misunderstand, Ms. Castellan." He met her gaze, holding it. "We're the ones asking the questions."

She studied him. Her gaze flicked to his sling, to his shoulder, and something flickered across her expression—something subtle. Satisfaction. Like she was proud of Gabriel.

"Gabriel was a troubled boy, Detective Muttler. A sick man." Livia spread her hands, almost in a gesture of helplessness. "I did what I could to protect society from him."

Johnson snorted. "By letting him roam free in your abandoned house?"

Livia's expression didn't shift. "Contrary to what you believe, Mr... I've forgotten your name."

"Johnson. Detective Johnson," he snapped.

A slow, amused smile spread across Livia's lips.

Clayton leaned in. "If you cared about your son, you would have done more than hide him like a dirty secret. Loved him and accepted him as a member of the family."

The air in the room changed.

Livia's fingers tightened slightly against the arms of her chair. For the first time, something rippled through her mask—a hint of something raw.

Then, she whispered:

"Do you have children, Detective?"

Clayton didn't blink. "No."

Livia inhaled sharply, her lips trembling just slightly. "Then you don't know what it is to raise them."

"No," Clayton said, standing slowly, gaze locked onto hers. "But I had a mother."

And then, with quiet finality— "Thank God she was nothing like you."

Livia's mask didn't break. Not completely. But something shifted in her eyes as Clayton turned for the door.

And for the first time, she had no response.

Clayton sat in the passenger seat of Johnson's Dodge Durango, wincing as they hit another bump in the road. His shoulder throbbed, the pain flaring each time the SUV jolted.

Johnson fiddled with the radio dial, cycling through static and half-played songs until he settled on something he liked. Within seconds, he was humming along, completely at ease.

Without looking away from the road—"You know she was talking shit, right?" Johnson's hands flexed on the wheel. "Gabriel Castellan had full access—13 Watt Avenue belongs to his mother. So does the lot next to Saint Michael's. And that bastard staged the bodies using the underground sewers."

Clayton exhaled through his nose. "Livia Castellan's too smart to take the fall for any of this." His voice was low, resigned. "She'll find a way to sweep it under the rug."

Johnson scoffed. "A serial killer son? No fucking way."

"You'd be surprised." Clayton leaned his head back against the seat.

A beat of silence passed. Then Johnson said, "You solved your first case, kid."

Clayton's eyes stayed closed, but his mind drifted—back three days, back to the moment he saw his own gun aimed at his face. The trigger pulled. The flash of muzzle fire. The sharp, searing pain in his shoulder.

And Johnson.

Clayton inhaled, grounding himself in the present. He had a lot to be grateful for.

Naomi

His father

Even Johnson.

"Thanks, man." His voice was quiet but firm. "Wouldn't be here if you didn't have my back."

Johnson didn't answer right away, but Clayton could tell he was smiling.

Finally—"You're alright, kid. You're alright."

Clayton didn't respond. He just kept his eyes closed, a small, tired smile on his lips as Johnson eased over the next bump in the road.

ABOUT THE AUTHOR

Gregory McEwan writes across genres, from dark fantasy and supernatural tales to modern detective novels and beyond. His stories span centuries and worlds, blending suspense, intrigue, and unforgettable characters.

OTHER BOOKS BY GREGORY MCEWAN

Clayton Muttler Detective Series

• *Anonyme* – Clayton Muttler's first major case uncovers dark secrets behind an exclusive dating service.

• *White Ravens* – A famed painting, two missing ravens, and a brutal murder challenge Clayton's detective skills.

• *Ink Runs Red* – Clayton races against time to stop a serial killer.

• *Final Debate* – Political intrigue and personal demons collide as Clayton solves his most high-stakes case yet.

The Immortal War Saga

• *The Vampire Larus: Clash of Clans* – The first book in the series, continuing the story introduced in *The Vampire Micah.*

• *The Vampire Micah* – The second book in the series, revealing Micah's origins and the ancient darkness that will shape his destiny.

The End

www.ingramcontent.com/pod-product-compliance
Lightning Source LLC
Chambersburg PA
CBHW020501310726
48979CB00016B/2746/J

* 9 7 8 1 0 6 9 6 7 0 6 9 4 *